JAIL BREAK

Edge and the three men in the jail snapped their heads around to look at a man who had seemed to fold himself off the front wall of the building to stand splay-legged in the doorway. He was aiming a double-barrel shotgun from the hip.

Both Edge and Larsen reached instinctively for their holstered revolvers.

"Pull them and everybody'll be just some sticky red stuff on the walls!" Two men suddenly came up from crouches outside the glassless window, both aiming guns. "Best get your hands up high," one of them growled menacingly.

Edge was wondering if there was any way he could possibly shoot fast enough to get out of this one . . .

THE EDGE SERIES:

#1 THE LONER
#2 TEN GRAND
#3 APACHE DEATH
#4 KILLER'S BREED
#5 BLOOD ON SILVER
#6 RED RIVER
#7 CALIFORNIA KILL
#8 HELL'S SEVEN
#9 BLOODY SUMMER
#10 BLACK VENGEANCE
#11 SIOUX UPRISING
#12 DEATH'S BOUNTY
#13 THE HATED
#14 TIGER'S GOLD
#15 PARADISE LOSES
#16 THE FINAL SHOT
#17 VENGEANCE VALLEY
#18 TEN TOMBSTONES
#19 ASHES AND DUST
#20 SULLIVAN'S LAW

#21 RHAPSODY IN RED
#22 SLAUGHTER ROAD
#23 ECHOES OF WAR
#24 SLAUGHTERDAY
#25 VIOLENCE TRAIL
#26 SAVAGE DAWN
#27 DEATH DRIVE
#28 EVE OF EVIL
#29 THE LIVING, THE DYING, AND THE DEAD
#30 TOWERING NIGHTMARE
#31 THE GUILTY ONES
#32 THE FRIGHTENED GUN
#33 RED FURY
#34 A RIDE IN THE SUN
#35 DEATH DEAL
#36 TOWN ON TRIAL
#37 VENGEANCE AT VENTURA
#38 MASSACRE MISSION

#38

EDGE

MASSACRE MISSION

BY

George G. Gilman

PINNACLE BOOKS   NEW YORK

EDGE #38: MASSACRE MISSION

Copyright © 1981 by George G. Gilman

A Pinnacle Books edition, published by special arrangement with New English Library, Ltd.

First printing, December 1981

ISBN: 0-523-41449-8

Cover illustration by Bruce Minney

Printed in the United States of America

PINNACLE BOOKS, INC.
1430 Broadway
New York, New York 10018

For G. D., who once aimed at a very vulnerable spot

MASSACRE MISSION

Chapter One

It had been a long ride from Ventura, Territory of Utah, to this spot on the bank of an arroyo in western New Mexico Territory which the man had chosen for a night camp. Not a hard ride, for he was in no particular hurry to get where he was headed, which was still a long way from here.

He stirred the ashes of the fire to life. The water in the pot was hot enough for shaving and to draw flavor from the coffee grounds before the false dawn was succeeded by sunrise. He was shaved, relishing a second cup of coffee and smoking the first cigarette of the day by the time the bright, hot sun was completely clear of the San Mateo Mountain ridges, some seventy miles away on the far side of the San Agustin Plains, which had taken him two days to cross.

He drank the coffee and smoked the cigarette sitting on his saddle, boots off but hat on.

1

Unused to luxury, the man enjoyed such small comforts in the early morning before the sun began its relentless climb toward unleashing the full punishing power of its summer heat.

Not that he showed any sign of pleasure, for he had the kind of face which, in repose, was totally impassive. A long, lean face, stained dark brown by heritage and close to forty years of exposure to the elements, deeply lined by the process of aging and the hardships he had survived during so many of those years. A face regarded by some as handsome but by many more as ugly. High cheekbones and a firm jawline flanked a hawklike nose; the narrow-lipped mouth could, by the merest movement, indicate the latent brutality within the man—and with another move could express a smile that most times was either cynical or sardonic, seldom warm. A smile that hardly ever touched the eyes—which during the waking hours were permanently narrowed under hooded lids—light blue in color, cold and penetrating in the way they viewed their surroundings.

Framing this face of a man who had obviously experienced more than his fair share of the harsh realities of life, was a mop of unkempt jet-black hair that concealed most of his forehead and grew long enough to brush his shoulders and veil the nape of his neck. Matching its color, but not its thickness, were the bristles he allowed to remain along his top lip and on either side of his mouth as little more than a suggestion of a moustache.

After pulling on his scuffed black riding boots, he unfolded his six-feet three-inch, close

2

to two-hundred-pound frame from the saddle and began his preparations to break the night camp. A man adequately attired and supplied for a lone ride over the empty, sun-baked landscape of the southwestern territories. Between the gray Stetson and the spurless boots, he wore a small-checked shirt and dark blue denim pants, with a gray kerchief not quite concealing the beaded thong that encircled his throat. It was from a pouch, held to the nape of his neck by this thong, that he had drawn the straight razor with which he had shaved. A razor that had often been used for purposes other than scraping the stubble from his face.

A more conventional weapon was the Frontier Colt which nestled in a holster hung low from the right side of his gunbelt and was tied down to his thigh. Likewise the Winchester rifle, which jutted from a forward-slung boot on the western-style saddle that he cinched to the back of his black gelding. The saddle was also supplied with a lariat, two canteens, and a pair of bags that contained enough water and food to last for a week. To the rear he lashed his bedroll with his eating utensils wrapped inside and a knee-length topcoat and rain slicker tidily stowed on top.

He used a foot to scrape dusty soil over the last glowing embers of the fire and asked of the big, solidly built gelding:

"You ready, horse?"

The animal scratched at the ground with a forehoof and tossed his head, venting a low snort. The man easily swung up astride the mount and ran the fingers of a brown-skinned

3

hand down the smoothness of the neck, heeled him gently in the flanks, and tugged on the reins to veer him across the arid, pebble-strewn bed of the arroyo. Today and for a few days more the going would be harder for the gelding: the man's destination of Tucson lay across the high ground of the Continental Divide. During the morning the rider allowed his mount a loose rein, only commanding a turn to left or right in order to take the easiest route around or over a natural obstacle, the animal setting his own pace in the steadily mounting heat.

Rest stops were made at hourly intervals, and at the steepest inclines or those composed of loose shale, the man dismounted to lead the animal by the reins. Every now and then as he rode, the man took the makings from a pocket of his shirt and rolled a cigarette, which he smoked in a leisurely, almost lazy manner—the way in which he appeared to do everything. But his apparant nonchalance as he rode, walked, or rested in this vast tract of outwardly empty rugged country was no more than a wafer-thin veneer cloaking his true attitude of constant vigilance. His slitted, glinting eyes maintained a distrustful watch on rocky ridges, dusty hollows, and widely scattered clumps of brush, while his lean but powerfully built frame was poised to react in an instant should danger strike—as it had so often struck at the half-Mexican, half-Scandinavian man called Edge.

But the morning passed as quietly as every other morning, afternoon, and night since he had ridden away from the violence at Ventura to reclaim this horse which had been stolen from him, and then head for Tucson, Arizona Territory, where he was in line to collect a reward of fifteen hundred dollars for a job he did not know he was going to get paid for. Killing three men.

At midday he found a patch of hot shade under an overhanging cliff face and ate a meal of cold beans and jerked beef washed down with tepid water. He watered his horse from his hat, and when the sun was a half-hour into its slow slide down the southwestern dome of the cloudless sky, he rose from where he had been squatting against the base of the cliff and drawled:

"Set to move again?"

This time the horse waved his head from side to side.

"Now don't you start to be a disagreeable animal, feller," the half-breed muttered. He spat out the taste of the stale water before getting astride the gelding and striking a match on his Colt butt to light the cigarette that angled from a corner of his mouth.

A long detour northwestward was necessary in order to reach the high ground above the cliff, where a section of the sandstone face had crumbled and left a boulder-strewn slope that offered a way to the top, provided the horse was not burdened with a rider.

Halfway up the three-hundred-foot-long, obstacle-laden grade, the gelding snorted his dislike for the climb as one of his hind hooves slid to the side, sending a shower of tiny rock fragments skittering downwards.

"Easy, feller," Edge said soothingly. He drew

his lips into a grimace as he coaxed the animal between two jagged boulders and saw that they had to negotiate some fifteen feet of steeply sloping, slightly curved ground, surfaced with crushed rock that was virtually shingle. "Real easy," he murmured, testing the treacherous ground with his own weight before gently tugging on the reins.

Minor avalanches were triggered by the setting down of booted feet and shod hooves, but man and horse slid not at all. And as they moved cautiously upward, the animal gained confidence, while tension, rather than the heat of the sun beating down on his back, squeezed beads of sweat from every pore in the half-breed's skin.

Then, as he reached out a hand to grip a projection of rock and began to haul himself up onto solid ground, he smiled fleetingly and jutted out his lower lip to blow a cooling draft of breath over his perspiring face.

"You vant some help, *mein herr*?"

There were still some seventy-five feet to the end of the climb when the foreign-accented voice shouted the offer. Perhaps the man at the top of the slope had not intended the words to be so loud, but they echoed between the rugged rock faces of the sloping gully, gaining both volume and stridency.

The gelding threw up his head. Edge swamped his initial impulse to snarl a curse. He realized it was too late to attempt soothing words to the horse: by bringing up his head, the gelding had altered the distribution of his weight on the unfirm ground. His hind legs slid; and in struggling to get surefooted again, more crushed rock was disturbed. His hind legs splayed and he snorted his panic as his fore-hooves sought to maintain a grip on the ground—and failed, causing more rock fragments to shower down the slope. Nostrils wide and eyes bulging, the gelding attempted to rear as he brought his hind legs together on apparently firm ground. He half rose and the reins were snatched from Edge's hand.

"Come on, feller, come on!" Edge rasped through gritted teeth, the words masked by the sound of the animal's terror and the clatter of rocks hurtling down the slope.

For an interminable second, as dust from the skittering rocks billowed into the air, it seemed as if the gelding would save himself. But then the ground beneath his left hind hoof crumbled, and he swung to the left with all his weight on his right leg.

Edge heard the man at the top of the gully shouting, though his voice was muffled. The snapping of a bone in the leg of the horse was as clear as a gunshot in the dead of night. The animal gave a shrill cry of agony as a point of starkly white cannon-bone pierced the flesh behind the fetlock and then was hidden by a gush of bright crimson. The animal ceased to flail at the air with his forelegs and crashed to the ground on his right side. He slid down the slope amid more falling rocks and came to rest between the two boulders, where the treacherous surface at once began and ended.

All was silence, except for the deep breathing of the horse, interspersed with low-keyed

7

whimpers. The dust settled and subdued the brightness of the trail of blood across the small rocks. There was no longer terror or even pain in the eyes of the stricken animal as he lay, head on the ground, gazing up at Edge. He seemed at once to be pleading for help and expressing some equine apology for failing the man who had cared for him so well until now.

"*Mein Gott*, vhat a terrible thing for the horse!" the man at the top of the gully gasped, the words little more than a whisper.

"Do something for me, feller?" Edge asked evenly, without looking toward the man.

"Anything, *mein herr*, that I can do to help you, I—"

"This is to help yourself, feller. Keep your mouth shut. Less chance of you talking yourself to death."

He started down the slightly curved slope as carefully as he had come up, anxious not to cause the injured horse more discomfort by kicking rocks against his head. Behind and above him the foreigner was muttering softly in his native language. His tone was plainly aggrieved.

Edge went down on his haunches beside the horse and merely glanced at the bloodstained bone protruding from the flesh of the leg. He reached out his left hand, and the gelding pressed his lips against the palm, pushing out his rough-textured tongue as if seeking a tidbit of food. The half-breed's right hand trembled for part of a second as he drew the Frontier Colt from its holster. There was implicit trust in the one eye Edge could see, as he rested the muzzle of the revolver on the animal's head after thumbing back the hammer.

"Guess you're ready to go now, feller?" the half-breed asked softly.

The gelding merely blinked his eye.

Edge squeezed the trigger and his hand moved not at all under the recoil. But his whole body trembled with the jerk of the animal's dying.

"You are blaming me for vhat has happened?" the man at the top of the gully called, nervously angry.

Edge said nothing. He slid the Colt back into the holster and knew at a glance there was no chance of taking the saddle off the gelding's carcass: it was wedged between the animal's back and one of the jagged rocks. But he was able to withdraw the Winchester from the boot, free the bedroll, and use the razor to cut loose one saddlebag and a canteen. Then, with this gear gathered under one arm, he turned and started back up the slope of the rock fall, needing to take the same care as before over the precarious stretch.

The man he had only so far glimpsed at the top of the gully was no longer there. But Edge could hear the sounds of his presence as he neared the end of the climb: mutterings in a foreign language, heavy footfalls, and the noises of a man in a great hurry to complete a chore. Close to the cliff top, just before he was in a position to see, Edge recognized the noises: the man was making haste to put a two-horse team into the traces of a wagon.

"You figuring to take off and leave me

9

stranded out here in the hills, feller?" the half-breed asked evenly, when he had achieved the level ground, some twenty feet from where the man was struggling clumsily to untangle harness.

The man whirled and made a move to delve his right hand toward something hidden by the left side of his suit jacket. But the sight of the tall, lean, glinting-eyed Edge, with the Winchester canted to his shoulder, caused the man to freeze like a figure carved from rock.

"*Mein herr,* mister . . . sir . . . I think you are . . ." Sweat like raindrops beaded on the skin of his pale face.

"Just plain Edge, feller."

The man blinked several times, then dropped the reaching hand to his side. He was about fifty, five and a half feet tall, and probably weighed close to a hundred and fifty pounds, the excess flesh evenly distributed over his rotund frame and thick limbs. His round, heavily jowled face was in keeping with his build. The pale green eyes, snub nose, and almost rosebud mouth all seemed too small for their setting. He was clean-shaven and had a smooth, unblemished complexion. The hair that showed below the brim of his gray derby hat was black and in the process of graying. The hat, dark gray city suit, shirt of pure white with a starched collar, red cravat, and black patent-leather shoes had all cost a lot of money in a smart store far back from the frontier.

While Edge slowly advanced toward him, the man's shirt collar became limper and began to turn gray with the salty moisture that dripped onto it from his fleshy jawline.

"Herr Edge, you made me afraid," the fat foreigner said quickly, gulping some hot afternoon air into his lungs. "I did not mean to cause . . . You threatened my life, did you not?"

Edge shifted his eyes along their narrowed sockets to glance at the man's rig. It was a timber-bodied merchant's delivery wagon, its seat covered by a forward projection of the roof of the enclosed rear. As citified as the man's garb, it showed more signs of being ravaged by the terrain and climate of the southwestern trails. But the expertly painted lettering on the side looked to be brand-new: FRITZ VON SCHEEL PURVEYOR OF BEAUTY TO LADIES.

"You're a long way from home, I figure," Edge said.

Von Scheel attempted an amiable smile that did not entirely conceal his nervousness. "*Ja*, I am from Germany. You will ride with me to Santa Luiz, Herr Edge?"

The half-breed went to the side of the wagon and tossed the bedroll, saddlebag, and canteen up onto the seat. He spat on a front wheel rim, and the saliva sizzled on the sun-baked metal. He kept the Winchester canted to his shoulder, but shifted his thumb to rest it on the rifle's hammer.

"The choice is yours, feller," he said.

Confusion became mixed with the German's apprehension.

"Whether or not to go for whatever kind of

11

gun you've got under your coat," Edge explained. "I either ride with you, or I ride alone. On account of how things are right now, you've got no way of making me walk."

Chapter Two

Fritz von Scheel started to protest that he had no intention of trying to abandon Edge. That he had been frightened by Edge's manner in the wake of the accident and had been prepared to defend himself against an attack.

"Just hitch the team," the half-breed interrupted, as he climbed up onto the seat of the wagon, without interrupting his apparently casual watch of the fat German. "And there's no rush. Far as I'm concerned."

Von Scheel smiled more brightly and used a red handkerchief to mop the sweat from his face before setting about untangling the harness—a man abruptly relieved of a great burden of doubt.

Edge watched him for a few moments as he started to roll a cigarette, then became aware of the cloyingly sweet smell emanating from behind him and peered through a glassless aperture into the wagon's body. In the light that fil-

13

tered through a crack between the two rear doors, he saw that the freight was composed of many white cardboard cartons, all labeled in a language he thought was French rather than German. A square of thick paper, folded several times, was wedged between two of the cartons close to the aperture. He pulled it free and unfolded it.

A military map, printed for the U.S. Army Department of New Mexico and rubber-stamped as the property of Department Headquarters, Fort Marcy, Santa Fe. The map was creased, torn, and stained from a great deal of use since its date of issue which was December 1865. Just as the recently painted sign on the side of the wagon stood out starkly against its drab and timeworn background, so a line of dashes in fresh red ink contrasted with the printed matter on the map. The marks followed a trail from Albuquerque to a point marked Mission of Santa Luiz in the vicinity of Fort West.

Edge struck a match on the stock of the Winchester as von Scheel climbed awkwardly up to the driver's seat and stabbed a pudgy finger at a point on the map some ten miles from where the marked route ended.

"Ve are here, Herr Edge. I intended to be much closer to my destination by this time, but the horses vere tired by the steep climb. And vhile they rested, I myself fell asleep. If you had not approached, I would perhaps still be sleeping."

The half-breed folded the map and inserted

14

it back where he had found it. "You figure to do good business beautifying women at a mission, feller?"

The German picked up the reins. "It is all right ve leave now?"

"It's your rig. I'm just along for the ride."

Von Scheel nodded and flicked the reins as he released the brake lever. "And I am pleased you are vith me. There are Apache Indians in this area. If there is trouble vith them, ve can protect each other, *Ja?*"

The wagon rolled forward, along a just discernible trail that followed the line of the cliff rim some twenty feet back from it.

"Your rig and team are all that appeal to me about you, feller."

The German scowled. "But ve are both vhite men, Herr Edge. Surely if hostile redskins attempted to halt us, you vould—"

"Do my damnedest to stay alive and make them regret they ever laid eyes on me. Guess San Luiz isn't just a mission anymore, uh?"

Von Scheel shot a sidelong look of disgust at Edge, then nodded and concentrated on the trail ahead. "That is right. I vas told in Santa Fe about this place. It vas left to decay many years ago by the Mexican priests after three of their number vere murdered by Apache Indians. Then, three years ago, some vhite people— Americans—came there. Sick people from the cities in the East. They came for the dry climate vhich is good for their health. Old people, you understand. Many more have come since those first ones."

15

"And old ladies are more in need of that sweet-smelling junk in the back than young ones," Edge added evenly.

A smile with overtones of avariciousness wreathed the fleshy face of the German. "There is no voman so vain as an old voman, *mein herr*. And also they have had more time in vich to accumulate vealth vith vich to buy my merchandise."

He glanced at Edge, the lack of whose response to his smiling goodwill caused it to fade.

"People may buy or not, as they choose. And it is an honest business I am in," von Scheel said quickly, defensively.

Edge wrinkled his nose and blew out a stream of tobacco smoke. "My opinion is your business stinks, feller."

"*Mein herr*, I carry only the finest perfumes and cosmetics manufactured by the best factories in Europe and—"

"Save the sales pitch for the old biddies down the trail," Edge cut in. He rested his booted feet on the top of the boarding in front of him and slid down into a more comfortable posture on the seat, tilting his hat forward so that its brim cast more shade over his eyes. "I ain't in the market for what you got to sell."

"I thought you vanted to talk," the driver snapped.

"Just about Santa Luiz, feller. And since you ain't been there before, don't figure you can tell me what I want to know about it."

"Vhat is that?"

"If there's a place there that sells horses."

"That I do not know, *mein herr*."

16

"Like I just said, I figured."

For a while, von Scheel seemed to be uneasy with the verbal silence as the horses clopped unhurriedly along the old trail, hauling the creaking wagon behind them. But then he became as content as his taciturn passenger with the lengthening pause in conversation, although he was far less philosophical about the dust raised by the horses and the sweat that the afternoon heat caused to stream down his face. He constantly brushed his jacket and pants, and mopped at his flesh with the handkerchief, often rasping low-keyed German curses at the causes of his irritation.

Edge surveyed the terrain over which they moved. They were away from the top of the escarpment now, rolling southwest along the barren bottom of a rocky valley, the monotony of the sandstone relieved here and there by clumps of dusty brush and the occasional cactus growing in stately isolation. Notable by their absence from the cloudless sky were buzzards, and the half-breed grimaced briefly as he considered an image of the ugly birds squabbling in their greed to tear and claw at the flesh of the horse's carcass, eager to gouge deeply inside the gelding and find the gory entrails.

"*Mein Gott,* an Apache Indian!" the German blurted suddenly, moving to snap the reins above the backs of the two horses.

Edge reached out his free hand and fastened it around one of von Scheel's wrists. "That one on the skewbald top of the valley to the right, feller?"

"*Ja!*"

17

"He's been shadowing us from ahead ever since we started through here. No sense in worrying unless him and a whole lot more get a deal closer."

Some of the tension eased out of the German with a sigh, and Edge released his hold on him. "You have experience vith the Indian race?"

"Had the occasional run-in with them. So far always came out winning. Except with the Sioux up in the Dakotas, I guess."

Von Scheel was spending more time looking up, squint-eyed, at the Apache brave riding along the top of the valley side than at the trail ahead.

"You drive, feller," Edge instructed evenly. "I'll take care of the shotgun end."

The German gave almost his full attention to keeping the team moving in the right direction, sparing just the occasional glance toward the Indian, who for a long time had made no secret of his presence.

"Vhat happened in the Dakotas? Vith the Sioux?"

"My business."

"But you spoke of it first!" von Scheel complained, irritated again.

Edge pursed his lips and blew between them. "Yeah, I did, didn't I? Got so used lately to only talking to a horse. He never asked questions."

The Sioux had been responsible for the horrifying death of Beth Hedges. At a time when the man called Edge was trying to revert to the identity he was born and bred to.

He had started out as an Iowa farm boy, and when the War Between the States shattered the

18

country, he fought for the Union, never certain if he would survive, but sure that if he did, he would return to the farmstead and continue to work it as before. But his ruling fates had dictated otherwise.

When former Captain Josiah C. Hedges of the Union Cavalry rode away from the the battlegrounds of the East, he was riding a trail that was destined to lead him into a west where he would never be able to forget the lessons of war—if he was to survive. His crippled kid brother Jamie had not learned such lessons, for he had been left at home to tend the farm. Alone—for the Hedges boys' parents were peacefully dead before the start of the war—so that when six of the meanest troopers to ride for the Union reached the farm ahead of the officer who had commanded them, the kid was more than simply outnumbered. He was also outclassed in depravity and brutality.

The buzzards were feeding on his corpse under the shadow of smoke rising from the burning farm buildings when Joe Hedges got home from the war. He found the killers of his brother, and he took his revenge for what they had done, using the lessons of a war that was ended. Because it was ended, this meant that a man who killed his enemy was no longer doing his duty: he was a murderer. In stepping outside the law, Josiah C. Hedges became the man called Edge, unable to return to his home.

Man-made justice never did catch up with him as he accepted his role as a drifter, but his ruling fates punished him to a degree worse than any hangman could have done. The trails he rode were seldom free of violence and death, deprivation and suffering. And, except for an occasional lapse, he came to accept that this was the way it would always be—life itself and the bare essentials for maintaining it were all he would ever have. To simply survive he would have to fight in peacetime more ferociously and with less compassion than during the war. But he now fought alone, though sometimes forming alliances of convenience—friendships that were doomed to end in anguish.

Then he met and married Elizabeth Day, and they set up house on a farm in the Dakotas not unlike the Hedges place in Iowa. Edge became Josiah C. Hedges again—and the difference went far deeper than a mere change of name. He knew from harsh past experience of the risks he was running in terms of the danger to Beth, and the anguish that would be his if his worst fear was realized. But as the days went peacefully by in the wake of their marriage, the tension eased. He had spat in the eye of those ruling fates, and it seemed they had admitted defeat this time. Or perhaps they had agreed that he had suffered enough for past misdeeds.

Then the Sioux came. And by the cruelest twist of all, he was made to feel responsible for the terrible way in which Beth died, a death that drained the last dregs of compassion for his fellow human beings out of him. Convinced that he was doomed to be a loner, he took the best life could offer whenever he could get it and cared not at all when the rewards were denied him: cold, impassive, brutal, and lacking in all ambition beyond the desire to survive.

"Mein herr," von Scheel said suddenly, as, close to the end of the valley, the Apache brave demanded a gallop from his pony and veered out of sight. "I have been thinking."

"It passes the time, feller."

"I have been thinking it vas my fault that your horse had the accident."

Edge nodded as he saw that the trail out of the valley curved in the same western direction in which the Apache had ridden and led into a forty-foot-wide ravine with steep sixty-foot-high walls: an ideal place in which to spring an ambush. "I figured that out when I saw him start to slide."

"I vill buy you a fresh horse, Herr Edge."

Another nod. "I'd decided that soon as he broke his leg."

The German scowled as he steered the creaking wagon around the curve of the trail, and spared just a quick glance for the half-breed before looking apprehensively up at the rims of the ravine walls. "Take care, *mein herr,*" he growled. "I am beginning to lose patience vith your attitude toward me."

"Hang on in there for a while, feller," Edge muttered, pointing toward a two-armed timber signpost set up at a fork in the trail. Black painted letters indicated, SANTA LUIZ 1m. through the ravine and THUNDERHEAD 5MS. along the southern spur.

The German obviously had weak eyesight because it was not until the wagon was passing directly by the signpost that he was able to read what was painted on it. And now he smiled avariciously. "Thunderhead vas not marked on the

21

map. But it is a very old map. Another town. More business. Is good."

The wagon rolled into the ravine where the heat of the day trapped between the walls felt more uncomfortable than out in the open valley. Von Scheel began to work harder at brushing the dust from his clothing and mopping the sweat off his face.

Edge sat up straighter on the seat and gripped the Winchester across his thighs a little more tightly, his narrowed eyes shifting from the tops of the flanking rock faces to the trail. The trail seemed to lead nowhere as it rose gently toward a partially obscured horizon of clear blue sky at the ravine's end, some two hundred yards away.

There was no ambush, and at the crest of the rise through the ravine, a broad panorama of solid terrain came into view, with Santa Luiz as its centerpiece.

The former Mexican mission was a little over a half-mile distant in the base of a dish of land encircled by sandstone ridges, with the tops of the ravine the highest points. There was a barren grandeur in the eroded formation of the surrounding hills and an incongruous beauty in what mankind had made of the settlement within them—aided by a ready supply of water from nature.

For water had to be plentiful to sustain the lush vegetation that was the first thing the two men aboard the wagon noticed about Santa Luiz. There was grass, trees that were not all native to the high desert country, and many patches of colorful flowering shrubs. The green

22

foliage and the multi-hued blooms contrasted pleasantly with the stark whiteness of the buildings.

The oldest and most weathered of these buildings, situated at the end of the trail over which the newcomers were approaching, was the mission church, a long and low structure, with a square bell tower at the eastern end. In front of it there was a broad plaza, flanked by newer buildings of the same adobe construction.

The largest patch of grass, to the north of the mission, featured several flourishing trees scattered at random, and two rows of neat white crosses to mark the graves of the dead. But each of the smaller buildings stood on a plot of land which had been more carefully cultivated, with lawns and flower beds out front and vegetable gardens to the rear.

There were ten of these houses along each side of the plaza, and as the wagon rolled closer, it could be seen that only half a dozen of them were recently built. The others were as old as the church but had been lovingly renovated.

"Vhere are all the people?" von Scheel muttered, nervous again, as he steered the wagon off the trail and onto the plaza, which had a grove of aspens at its center and rustic benches placed in their shade.

"They're around," the half-breed answered softly, aware of the signs of much movement on the dusty surface of the plaza. He spat into the dust. "Seems they don't have much use for horses, though."

A great many booted feet had left impressions on the ground. There were few hoofprints, all of which had been made by unshod animals. The German reined in the team beside the aspens and asked raspingly out of the corner of his mouth, "So vhere are they?"

He looked intently in every direction, even leaning to the side to peer back at the trail sloping down from the ravine. While Edge, who had a well-honed instinct for such things, gazed unblinkingly at the closed doorway in the base of the church bell tower.

"I'm here to buy and he's come to sell!" the half-breed shouted.

After the wagon had come to rest, a total silence descended over Santa Luiz and the surrounding countryside. All that moved for what seemed endless seconds were shadows, lengthening to the dictates of the sinking sun in the late afternoon sky. Edge's loud and sudden announcement triggered a gasp of shock from the throat of von Scheel. Less audible was a series of smaller sounds, made by the equally startled people gathered in the church.

"Nothing else!" the tall, lean man added less stridently, as he half rose and easily jumped down off the wagon. He canted the Winchester to his shoulder and reached up to get the rest of his gear.

There was talk inside the church now, enough to capture the attention of the German drummer. "I do not like this," he said tensely.

"They know how you feel," Edge told him, and then both of them looked across a hundred feet of plaza as the door of the church creaked open.

Three elderly men shuffled over the threshold, unarmed, their wrinkled faces showing the same brand of nervousness which had moments before gripped von Scheel. For a few seconds, while the old-timers and the strangers to Santa Luiz eyed each other, a subdued but constant splashing of falling water could be heard from within the church.

"Iffen that's the truth, then welcome here," the tallest and thinnest of the old men said. "Though us folks ain't in need of anythin' to buy. Ain't got much of anythin' to sell, either."

"You men'd be better off goin' to Thunderhead," the old-timer with a pronounced limp in his left leg advised coldly. "If it's business you're after doin'."

"Come mornin', Lloyd," a woman said quickly, as she emerged from the church doorway and swung around the trio of men to bustle toward the wagon, a bright and friendly smile on her sallow face. "It's a long ways from anywhere to here, so I reckon you young fellers are mighty weary. Be fed and housed by us for the night and go to that awful place refreshed tomorrow."

"That is most kind of you, *mein frau*," von Scheel responded effusively, as he clambered awkwardly down from the same side of the wagon as Edge. When he was on the ground, he clicked his heels together and bowed stiffly from the waist. "I, Fritz von Scheel, vill most certainly accept your generous invitation."

25

The tension and hostility that Edge had sensed emanating from inside the church when he first became aware that people were gathered there, had virtually dissipated by the time the seventy-year-old woman reached the wagon. She was girlishly flattered when the German took her right hand, raised it, and kissed it. But then a man shouted a single word, and a rifle shot shattered the burgeoning atmosphere of trust, which so briefly dispelled the suspicion that had apparently settled over Santa Luiz.

The bullet came closest to tunneling through the flesh of the gray-haired old woman, as it whizzed over her thin shoulder and then sped between Edge and von Scheel before it buried itself in the plaza with a puff of disturbed dust.

Edge did not have to see where the lead came to rest in order to get a line on the point from which it was fired. For as he watched the people emerging from the church in the wake of the old woman, he had glimpsed a spurt of gray muzzle smoke through the east-facing aperture at the top of the bell tower. Recognizing it for what it was, he had dropped his gear and was in the process of bringing the Winchester down from his shoulder before the report sounded.

On the periphery of his vision, as exclamations of shock were voiced from many throats, he saw the German hurl away the old woman's hand and throw himself into the cover of the nearest team horse as he reached under his coat.

"Get down, lady!" he snarled.

The woman, terror supplanting the shock which had swept away the smile, was about to turn around and run for the church. The half-breed took a single long stride toward her and hooked his leading foot to one of her ankles. His body went rigid, his rifle aimed and cocked, as she fell hard to the ground with a cry of alarm and pain.

The head, shoulders, and arms of a man showed at the opening high in the tower, and a second gunshot sounded, this time from the plaza and close to where Edge stood. Adobe chips flew away from a hole halfway up the tower. Edge squeezed the trigger of the Winchester, and the crack of the rifle's firing curtailed the German curse that von Scheel had started to mouth when the bullet from his handgun went so wide of the mark.

The glinting slits of the half-breed's ice-blue eyes were obscured momentarily as he blinked in reaction to the gunshot. But his thin lips remained slightly drawn back to display his teeth in a cruel smile, as he fired the shot with confidence and watched its result with satisfaction.

The bullet went into the head of the man in the tower, and he was jerked backward and upward from his crouch. His hands loosened their grip on his rifle, and it dropped, bounced on the ledge of the aperture, and went spinning down the outside wall to land with a thud on the ground beneath. By this time the man with the bullet in his head was on his feet—and on the brink of death. By flailing his arms he managed to keep from tottering backward. Then, as he died, the final movement of his arms caused his limp corpse to fall forward. He folded over the ledge, teetered there for a moment, and then followed the path of his rifle. Only now was it possible to see for certain that he was an Apache brave.

The silence intensified in the wake of the dull thud of the body crashing to the ground in the shadow of the church until Edge broke it by pumping the lever action of the repeater, ejecting the spent cartridge case and jacking a fresh round into the breech. "Which one of us, feller?" he asked von Scheel.

"Vhy you, of course," the fat German answered. "I had no chance at all with this." He displayed the small Smith and Wesson .32 revolver with which he had tried to shoot the Apache over such an impossible range.

"I mean which one of us was the brave trying to kill." Edge explained, nodding toward the bullet hole in the ground.

Von Scheel shrugged his shoulders, but the disinterested gesture was belied by the nervous way in which he licked his lips and shot a glance toward the crowd—some of whom were Apaches—gathering around the dead brave. "Vhy should an Indian vish to kill me, *mein herr*? An innocent salesman of perfumes and such to vomen?" He moved forward, pushing the small revolver into a shoulder holster and stooping to help the old lady to her feet.

Edge took a bullet from a loop on his gunbelt and pushed it through the loading gate of the Winchester. "Indians are kind of superstitious. Maybe that one didn't like the trick you do."

"Trick, *mein herr?*"

The half-breed canted the rifle to his shoulder and picked up the rest of his gear. "Turning *scents* into dollars."

Chapter Three

One of the recently built adobe houses was still vacant and the old lady Edge had knocked to the ground assured the newcomers it would be all right for them to spend the night there. She was recovered from the shock and the fall and was eager to thank the half-breed for his good intentions. Unlike her, the majority of the fifty or so people who had been hiding in the church were obviously resentful in the wake of the killing and unaware of exactly what had caused the sudden explosion of violence in this idyllic setting.

Edge said, "No sweat, ma'am, and I'm obliged," then angled back across the plaza to the house on the southeast corner. Fritz von Scheel went with the woman to help in explaining to the ignorant that it had been the Apache brave who fired the first shot.

Edge went up a walkway of crushed rock between the two flower-bedded rectangles of

31

lawn and through a doorway into a small parlor that was bare of furnishings and filled with the smells of fresh construction. To either side of the fireplace was a door: the one on the right leading to a kitchen and the one on the left to a bedroom. The latter was as bare as the parlor, but in the kitchen were some closets, a stove, and a sink with a pump behind it. The water from the pump was cool, clear, and sweet tasting. Edge drank at least a quart, and after so many days of sipping from canteens, it went down better than any beer.

Outside, as the leading arc of the sun touched the ridges to the southwest, the voices became fewer and less shrill. The half-breed went to the glassless window beside the front door of the house and grunted in approval when he saw that the German was in the process of taking the two-horse team from the traces of the wagon. Elsewhere, people were moving toward other houses, leaving a group of half a dozen in muffled conversation in front of the church. Five Apaches disappeared from sight around the side of the church, two of them carrying the dead brave by the ankles and armpits.

Among the white citizens of Santa Luiz, none was less than fifty and most appeared to be in the sixty-to-eighty age group. White-haired or bald, slight of frame and with time-lined faces, many of them were pained by the simple exertion of walking. Some of the more able-bodied were pale and haggard, showing the symptoms of a sickness that attacked internal organs rather than muscles. The men were attired in sweat-stained shirts, battered hats, creased and dirty pants, and scuffed boots, the women in shapeless, drab dresses, as stained and dirt-streaked as the men's clothing, their hair hanging limply around their wearied faces.

Some of these women eagerly eyed the sign painted on the side of the German's wagon, while a few of the men looked with animosity toward the house on the southeast corner of the plaza. Among the latter, only those with failing eyesight did not spot Edge's impassive figure at the window, and so did not look hurriedly away.

Then, from the rear of the church, came the sound of unshod hooves. At first it was a confusion of sound, until a gallop was called for, and Edge saw six ponies streaming up the northwest slope. Five had riders, while the one at the rear, on a lead line, was draped with the dead Indian over its back.

After the sounds of the Apaches had faded from earshot, the group of oldsters moved away from the front of the church. One of them veered away from his fellows to go to talk with von Scheel, who nodded, clicked his heels, and surrendered his horses to the man. The animals were led toward the rear of the church, and their owner hurried to get to the once vacant house ahead of the group.

Edge had rolled and lit a cigarette by this time.

"The men vish to speak vith us, Herr Edge," the German announced as he entered the house, where the air within the adobe walls was pleasantly cool relative to that out on the plaza.

"Always have been a better listener than a talker, feller," the half-breed answered, and turned to rest his rump on the window ledge as the deputation of oldsters came across the threshold. The gimpy-legged Lloyd was among them, the shortest of the group and, at about sixty, the youngest.

"This here's Lloyd DeHart," the tall, thin man who had offered a qualified welcome when the newcomers arrived said with a wave of a skinny, misshapen hand. "I'm Phil Frazier. John Newman over there. Arnie Prescott and Elmer Randall. Elmer's the husband of Amelia Randall who you knocked over out there awhile back."

"You done it to keep Amelia from danger, I know that," the stooped, thickly moustached, morose-eyed Randall said quickly.

One of Frazier's coal-black eyes was so bright it had to be made of glass. And its lid never blinked. Newman had a gray goatee and features that were almost skeletal. Prescott's skin coloration was unhealthily crimson, and he needed a stick to compensate for a right clubfoot. With the exception of Randall, each man gave a curt nod as he was named. Von Scheel made one click of his heels serve as a response to all of the introductions.

Edge said, "Should I be as glad to know you as you are me?"

Elmer Randall was characteristically morose. The other four expressed various degrees of sourness.

The German frowned at the half-breed and then smiled at the five old-timers when he said,

34

"Fritz von Scheel at your service, gentlemen. This is Herr Edge. Ve met on the trail."

DeHart ignored the drummer and was impatient with him to be done talking. He massaged the thigh of his left leg as if it pained him and growled, "Without 'Pache labor, we ain't got a cat's chance in a dog pound to get this place finished."

"Ve vere forced to defend ourselves against an unprovoked attack, *mein herr*!" von Scheel protested.

"Quit it, Lloyd," Frazier muttered, and his single natural eye shared a look of resignation equally between Edge and the drummer. "Ain't no doubt the Injun took a potshot at you men. And ain't no way we're ever gonna find out the reason he done that unless some of his buddies knows it and fixes to tell us."

"If I can buy a horse, I'll be on my way, feller," Edge offered.

"We ain't got no horses, mister," John Newman said. "On account of no one hereabouts is fit enough to ride."

Frazier shook his head. "Ain't no rush for you men to leave Santa Luiz. Them live Injuns'll be takin' the dead one to bury up on the Gallo Rancheria. Twelve hours there and twelve hours back. So you'll be okay restin' up here for the night. Advise you to leave in the mornin' though. For your own good. On account that I don't reckon Chief Ahone is gonna take too kindly to one of his brave's gettin' shot by a white."

"Ain't the army riding herd on the Rancheria, feller?" Edge asked.

Frazier shrugged.

DeHart growled. "A bunch of boys in blue ride up there from Fort McRae every once in a while. Have a smoke on the peace pipe and—"

"Things have been fine with the Indians for a long time," Arnie Prescott interrupted. "The Rancheria's on good land and there's an honest agent up there. Ahone's a good chief. Got vision. Knows reds and whites have got to get along together. Happy to have his braves work for us."

"Indians is Indians," DeHart muttered sourly. "Especially 'Paches."

"We going to put that to the vote?" Edge asked, and tossed the remains of his cigarette out of the window.

Frazier sighed and shared a glare between DeHart and Prescott. "Yeah, you men quit it, uh? The meetin's already been held out front of the church and we carried the motion." Now he directed his attention at the two newcomers. "And I guess you folks have got the drift of what the town council decided. Lousy thing that happened out there just now. But the milk's been spilt and everyone's got to make the best of it. And we reckon it's best if you folks take off soon as you're rested up. Santa Luiz folks gotta stay in Santa Luiz and hope Ahone's as good a chief as Arnie claims. Understands the killin' of one of his braves was nothin' to do with us."

"That is fair," von Scheel agreed.

"Be horses for sale at Thunderhead?" Edge asked.

"Them gold grubbers over there bought our

36

animals," John Newman answered, and was gripped by a racking fit of coughing that seemed to rattle the bones of his emaciated frame.

"Most likely ate them by now," the soured Lloyd DeHart added.

"Reckon you'll be able to get what you need, mister," Phil Frazier told Edge, as he signaled for the old-timers to leave the house. "But they're hard folks at Thunderhead. Drive hard bargains."

"No sweat, feller. I'll do the trading. Him the paying."

After the rest of the town councillors had left, Frazier held back to look with his good eye at the impassive Edge and then the piqued von Scheel. "Appears you folks don't get along too well together. Surely would appreciate it if any differences you got to settle can wait until you leave Santa Luiz. It's the peace and quiet as well as the clean air and the fine spring water us old folks come here for. And there's some among us liable to keel over and die iffen they get too agitated. You folks know what I mean?"

"I understand," the German said. "It is painfully known to many that old age does not come alone, *mein herr*."

Edge straightened up from the window ledge and rasped the back of a hand over the bristles of his jawline. "To others it doesn't come at all."

Frazier limped out of the house, and his shadow was cast long by the final rays of the setting sun. By the time he and the other members of the town council had gone into various houses on both sides of the plaza, the darkness had almost gathered to full night. The mingled aromas of wood smoke, cooking food, and bubbling coffee were appetizingly discernible in the cooling air. Lamplight began to show at many windows. Myriad stars gleamed hard and bright against the black sky. A quarter moon hung like half a question mark above the jagged ridges to the north.

Von Scheel stood in the doorway as he watched night fall. Edge unfurled his bedroll in a corner of the parlor, then sat on the blankets and unfastened the saddlebag. The German heard the small sounds he made and turned to look across the wanly moonlit room at him.

"The man who attended to my horses said ve vould be given hot food, Herr Edge."

"Jake Donabie said what I told him to," Amelia Randall announced, as her footfalls sounded on the crushed rock walkway. "The Lord knows that Santa Luiz folks don't have much, but it'd be a sad day when some of us weren't ready to share what we have with the needy."

She bustled into the house bearing a cloth-draped tray and surrendered it to von Scheel.

"*Danke.*"

"Obliged," said Edge.

"Just last night's mutton stew warmed up. More beans than meat but there oughta be enough to fill you folks's bellies. Eat hearty now."

She turned to leave, but paused in the doorway, looking with something less than her former demonstrative hospitality to where the German had set down the tray on the floor and pulled off the cover to reveal two deep bowls,

38

filled to their brims with steaming, aromatic stew.

"There is something you vish from us?" von Scheel asked, as he rose with a bowl and a spoon in hand.

"Me and some of my neighbors been talkin', mister. About the line you travel in."

A bright smile spread over the German's face, and in the dim light the overtones of avariciousness could not be seen.

Edge claimed the tray and returned to his bedroll to sit cross-legged while he began to eat the good-tasting stew.

"It vill be a great pleasure for me to show my vares to the ladies."

The elderly woman's uneasiness increased. She cast an apprehensive glance out at the empty plaza, allowing her attention to linger on the wagon parked beside the aspen grove. She asked softly, "Guess what you got to sell costs a lot?"

"My price range is vide, *mein frau*," the drummer answered. "But I vill make special concessions for you and your neighbors. Bargain prices for anything you vish to buy. In return for the hospitality vhich has been given to me and my traveling companion."

He no longer seemed hungry as he launched into his initial sales pitch, only to be disconcerted by Mrs. Randall's unenthusiastic reaction. "A good deal, this I promise you," he pressed on.

"It ain't that," the woman assured. "I ain't thinkin' you'd cheat us or nothin' like that. It's

39

just that if the men folk hereabouts found out about it, they wouldn't allow it. Us women spendin' money on what they figure as foolishness. So we'd have to do it real late in the night when the men's all asleep and snorin'. And be real quiet about it."

The smile reappeared on the drummer's fleshy features. "I am at your service. Vhen you say the time is right for us to do business, you come here again. And ve vill be as quiet as the mice, *Ja?*"

Now the woman smiled, nodded, and glanced again at the wagon as a giggle bubbled up from deep inside her. If her age-wearied legs had allowed it, she would doubtless have skipped down the walkway.

Von Scheel began to eat the stew, still standing, and when he was finished, the sigh of satisfaction he vented probably owed as much to the prospect of making money as to the warm fullness of his belly. "Did I not say it, *mein Herr* Edge?" he murmured with subdued delight. "The older the voman, the more she yearns for beauty."

Edge set the tray down on the floor and pushed it away. Then, forming his folded topcoat into a pillow, he got under his bedroll blankets, tipped his hat forward over his face, and muttered into the sweat-smelling darkness of its crown, "Yeah, feller. Figure it's in their makeup."

For a few minutes he was conscious of sounds and movements both within the adobe house and outside. He knew that von Scheel gathered up the dirty dishes, placed them on the tray by the door, then left to go to his wagon and returned with a burden. It was his bedroll, which he unfurled. When the German went into the kitchen and started to wash up, whistling softly through his teeth, the half-breed drifted into an easy sleep. It was briefly disturbed when his sharply honed subconscious warned of an intruder. But he only came to the threshold of waking, the fingers of his left hand tightening around the frame of the Winchester that shared his bedding. A woman was speaking with the German drummer. The talk was brief and low-keyed, but in tones of pent-up excitement. Then the two moved softly out of the house, closing the door behind them. The half-breed sank back into his brand of shallow but restful sleep again, against a background of more whispered talk and padding footfalls that entered from the plaza through the glassless window.

A loud and urgent shout jerked the sleeping man into full consciousness. He was instantly in control of his reflexes and commanded total recall of where he was and why he was there.

Leather cracked. Horses snorted. The half-breed recognized the voice of Fritz von Scheel shouting again. Hooves beat on the ground and timbers creaked. Edge was sitting upright by then, but did not hurry to get to his feet and move to the window, hat back squarely on his head and rifle canted casually to his shoulder.

The leaves of the aspens were trembling. A dust cloud was billowing. The windows of many houses became squares of yellow lamplight. Men and women shouted questions, which for the most part went unanswered—

except by the sight of the city-style wagon being driven in a tight, listing turn around the grove of trees, then heading out onto the trail that led up the eastern slope toward the ravine.

Edge stoically watched the frenetic departure of the German drummer, and when the sounds of the galloping horses and fast-rolling wagon had faded from earshot, could make sense of some of the questions and answers being yelled from house doorway to doorway.

". . . foreigner take off on his own?"

"Just saw the one guy up on the seat!"

"Wonder why he's in such an all-fire rush?"

"Get away from the tall, mean one, maybe!"

"Hush your mouth, Jonas!"

"Afeared of the Injuns is my guess!"

"No skin offen our noses, you folks! Let's all get back to bed for some more sleep!"

"Damn good idea!"

"Language, Ed!"

A few more phrases were muttered. Then doors were closed and lamps were doused. Far across the mountain ridges to the west, a coyote howled at the moon. When its echo had died away, the high country became silent. And the half-breed moved away from the window, intending to bed down again. But something white at the foot of the door caught his eye, and he crossed to pick it up: a folded sheet of paper from which several bills fell. He retrieved these—a five and six ones—before he opened the door to read by the moonlight what was written on the paper.

Herr Edge:

I had no money when I came to Santa Luiz. This is all I made from sales to the women here. You may ask them about this if you doubt me. Maybe you can buy a horse for this. If you cannot, I feel it is enough to discharge my debt for the contribution I made to the accident which befell your horse. I leave now so that I may be far away from here when the Apache Indians come. A man traveling as I am cannot travel fast. Auf Wiedersehen.

Fritz von Scheel.

"Guess it'll have to do, feller," Edge murmured, pushing the bills into a hip pocket, then screwing the note up into a ball and tossing it into a corner of the room.

Following a hunch, he crossed to go into the bedroom and saw that the drummer had been so anxious to depart without hindrance that he had chosen to leave his bedroll rather than risk arousing the suspicion of his fellow house guest. Edge claimed it and added it to his own, so that the remainder of the night was spent more comfortably.

He rose at first light and shaved with the razor from his neck pouch, used to the lack of a mirror and able to scrape off the bristles by touch without cutting into the line of his Mexican-style moustache. A faint trace of wood smoke flowed in through the windows on the cool morning air.

A tentative knocking on the door brought him back into the parlor just as Amelia Randall entered carrying an empty cup and a fire-blackened pot, giving off coffee-smelling steam. She was attired in the same shapeless dress as yesterday, but her face had a well-scrubbed look and her gray hair was neat and shiny from brushing.

"Figured you'd be wantin' to make an early start, young man," she said. "Won't be fixin' breakfast for my Elmer for a while yet."

"Obliged to you," he told her, as he took the pot and cup and poured himself a coffee. Smiling, he said, "Figure you and some of the other women will be making real good breakfasts this morning."

She shrugged her thin shoulders, then showed a smile of her own. "I reckon we will." She leaned against a doorpost. "Our men folk will be mad anyways. But there ain't nothin' they can do about it now. We got our fancy perfumes and paints and powders, and the drummer that sold them to us is long gone with the money."

"Hard-saved money, I guess?" He had sipped half the coffee, and now he dropped onto his haunches to begin furling his bedroll.

She sighed. "That's true enough, young man. Don't suppose there's any of us Santa Luiz folks had easy lives. And a lot of us got sick workin' so hard. But the clean air up here in the mountains and whatever kind of stuff is in the water springs inside the church is worth every cent we pay for it."

"Who do you pay, ma'am?"

She shook her head. "Not pay like that, young man. Folks that come here from the cities have to pledge all they got to the town. So

44

we can have supplies hauled in. Grub for the table and lumber and suchlike to build new places for new folks who want to come. Pay the Apaches for takin' care of the heavy buildin' work. A travelin' man comes here twice or maybe three times a year sellin' clothes and shoes. He was by a few weeks ago, and it was money we had left over from buyin' from him that we used for dealin' with that foreigner."

She sighed again as she scanned the plaza with the first shaft of the new day's sun falling across it. "First luxury we've had since we got here—not countin' better health, of course. Foolishness, I know, and we'll get bawled out for doin' what we done. But old as us biddies are, we're still women. And there's more to bein' one of them than cookin' and cleanin' house for a man. And when the men folk get through with yellin' at us, I guess we'll figure it was worth it. When we sit in front of our lookin' glasses and get started at tryin' to paint out the wrinkles and usin' the fancy perfumes to cover up the stink of old age."

Edge had packed his gear, and now he finished the cooled coffee at a swallow and refilled it from the pot. Then he took a dollar from his hip pocket and pushed it through the handle of the pot.

"What's that for?" Mrs. Randall asked.

The half-breed gestured with the cup. "This and the stew last night, ma'am. Always pay for what I have."

"There ain't no need, young man."

"For me there is."

"Suit yourself."

"Usually do."

She nodded. "So it suited you for the drummer to take off on his own last night? I saw you standin' at that window just watchin' him."

"He was nothing but a ride to me, ma'am. And if I'm going to have to dodge fired-up Apaches, I figure the chances are better on foot than aboard his rig." He finished the second cup of coffee and hurled the dregs out through the window.

"It could be there won't be trouble from the Indians," the woman suggested, as she took the empty cup from him and picked up the pot with the dollar bill through the handle. "That brave you shot; I'm not so sure he's one of Chief Ahone's people from the Gallo Rancheria."

Edge raised his gear from the floor. "How's that, ma'am?"

"Ain't none of us folks hereabouts ever laid eyes on him before. And we seen a lot of Apaches from Gallo. Come down here in bunches of five or six at a time and set up camp out back of the church. Nice, quiet, friendly folks—most of them. For Apaches. Carry knives and them tomahawk things, but only to work with.

"That one you killed . . . he come ridin' into Santa Luiz last evenin' yellin' at our workers fit to bust. One of our workers, he says this brave has seen two whites headin' for town. That maybe there'll be trouble and we oughta be ready.

"Well, we don't have no guns. Never did have need of them here. So we all goes into the church. To hide and wait to see what's gonna happen. Never did see the goin' of the Apache that caused the scare. Until he was layin' dead there under the bell tower. Seems some of the men folk tried to get our workers to tell us why the strange Apache tried to shoot somebody. But they just shut up tight as clams."

Edge grinned, but his narrowed and glinting eyes remained mirthless. "Figure that sounds fishy, ma'am."

"Amelia!" the morose-faced husband of the woman yelled angrily from three houses down the south side of the plaza. "Amelia, where are you, woman? Where's the coffeepot?"

She sighed. "Pity you're leavin'," she said wearily. "Elmer always has been somethin' of a bear with a sore head first thing mornin's. But pretty soon I reckon you'd be the only good-tempered man in Santa Luiz."

She stepped out on to the walk and called to her husband that she was on her way. Edge followed her. "Oh," she remembered. "Since you ain't ridin' the wagon, quickest way to Thunderhead is to cut through the hills." She pointed south between two of the houses. "Ain't such easy goin' as on the trail, but a lot shorter for a man on foot or horseback."

Edge flicked the underside of his hat brim with a forefinger and answered, "Obliged to you, ma'am."

As the woman returned to the house she shared with her husband, he started in the direction she indicated. The sun was fully risen above the eastern ridges now and already beginning to feel hot on a man's face. Once he and the woman had stepped off the plaza, it

47

was empty, but several chimneys of the flanking houses were sending up wisps of wood smoke as evidence that many of the elderly health-seeking citizens of Santa Luiz were up and about. In the tranquillity of the early morning, the trickle of running spring water was just discernible from within the mission church.

But the tall, lean half-breed did not have to trudge very far up the sloping ground to the south of the small community before the setting down of each booted foot provided the only sound he could hear. Just a few yards in back of the gardens of the adobe houses, the land was parched and dusty, and a man with a less imaginative streak than Edge might have needed to look over his shoulder to remind himself of the well-tended gardens and the shade trees, which made Santa Luiz a virtual oasis in the high country desert. But he did glance back when he was almost to the top of the slope, about a mile distant from the community.

Thirty minutes had elapsed by then, and in that time the sick and crippled inhabitants of the former mission had started the chores that were necessary to hold back the desert from the place: moving in and out of the church with pails and sprinkling cans to draw water from the spring, which they poured onto the thirsty ground wherever any greenery grew. It was hard work for such elderly people, and painful for those with age-stiffened or diseased joints. But, Edge reflected as he shifted his impassive gaze to the south again, such tasks filled the oldsters' time and gave purpose to the lives they sought to prolong by coming here. So there was neither cynicism nor pity for the old people in the half-breed's train of thought. For if there was purpose to their lives, they were better off than he was.

Suddenly a man ordered, "Halt!"

Edge complied, bringing his trailing foot forward and freezing to the spot where he stood in the early morning shade of a rock outcrop on the crest of the rise.

"Drop rifle. Then take revolver from holster and also drop."

The man giving the orders was twenty feet above him, on the top of the outcrop. He spoke American with a more pronounced accent than Fritz von Scheel. But even before Edge had let go of the Winchester, then taken the Colt from his holster and dropped it to the ground, he knew the man on the rock was as American as they come. For he had recognized the guttural tones of an Indian.

He tilted his head back to look up at the Apache brave, who showed just his head, shoulders, and one hand and arm against the bright blueness of the sky—the hand fisted around the butt of a Navy Colt.

"You do good to do as I say, white eyes."

The half-breed shifted his unemotional gaze from the single brave to a line of ten more, who were riding their ponies out of a dip some hundred yards to the right on the southern slope. "You weren't expected until nightfall," he drawled evenly as the riders advanced slowly up the slope, each grim-faced and carrying a rifle or carbine, butt resting on a thigh and barrel angled skyward.

"And from the north the white eyes think we will come," the Apache who was sprawled out on his belly at the top of the outcrop said. "To do always what is expected is unwise." The mounted braves reined in their ponies ten feet away from Edge. "But now you will be very wise if you do as I expect and go with my brothers back to the place where the elders live."

Edge looked up at the lone brave and then back at those astride the ponies, as the rifles and carbines were leveled at him. He rasped, "Easy. Intend to do what's expected of me."

Chapter Four

As the half-breed turned and started back down the slope toward Santa Luiz he felt no self-anger at having allowed the Apaches to get the drop on him. Any brave worthy of the name, who discovered a white man out in the open and clearly unsuspecting of the presence of hostile Indians in the immediate area, would always take the advantage of surprise. What Edge did feel, though, was fear. An ice-cold fear that required considerable effort to confine to the pit of his stomach.

On the high ground to the north of Santa Luiz, he saw other Apaches riding their ponies and starting down the decline at the same slow but relentless pace that the fact of his walking necessitated.

It had been a necessarily fast yet a coolly taken decision to submit to the demands of the Apache on the rock, and he had made it on the assumption that the brave was not alone—that any attempt to retaliate would invite certain death. Of course he had been right, but what more had he achieved than another mere quota of borrowed time?

The Indians had not wanted to gun him down out of hand. So what then did they have in mind for their prisoner who the day before had killed one of their tribe? These Apaches on the southern hill and those to the north were, with a single exception, all similarly attired in buckskin pants and waistcoats with single feathers in headbands. Some were barefooted, others wore moccasins, a few favored decorative necklaces and arm bands, and all—again excepting the distinctively dressed Indian, toted a rifle or a carbine.

This singular man, who rode at the center and slightly to the front of the score or so Indians on the northern hill, was obviously the chief. He was dressed like a white man, in a store-bought suit that had once been white, and a black Stetson hat. His riding boots were also black, as was the string tie that was fastened around his throat. Nevertheless, he wore no shirt.

Long before the two groups of Apaches got close enough for Edge to notice such details about the chief's clothing, the morning chores in Santa Luiz had come to a premature end. The shouts of alarm that arose when the old-timers first spotted the advancing Indians had been followed by a tense silence, while wives sought the reassuring closeness of their husbands, and couples quickly formed groups all over the plaza.

Edge and his escort reached the shade of the aspen grove moments ahead of the Indians coming from the other direction, and he was immediately aware of a mixture of hostility and sympathy directed toward him from his fellow whites. A few of the old-timers nodded, smiled tentatively, or forced a bright greeting for those of the braves who had done some work in renovating and expanding the former mission. But there were no responses from the dour Apaches.

It was the half-breed who called the halt, when he had reached the aspens and seated himself on one of the rustic benches, setting his bedroll, saddlebag, and canteen down beside him. He took out the makings and began to roll a cigarette with practiced ease, while he watched the Apache who was outfitted like a white man lead his group between the houses on the north side of the plaza.

There was a flurry of voices and movement out front of the church, and a great many guns were raised toward its source. These were lowered when the Indians saw and recognized the tall, thin, one-eyed Phil Frazier wrenching himself free of the hold a woman had on him and striding purposefully toward the chief.

Lloyd DeHart, as usual favoring his left leg, was the first to move up alongside Frazier, followed by John Newman, fingers combing his pointed gray beard. The crimson-complected Arnie Prescott and the stockily built, totally bald Jake Donabie advanced together to bring the group to five. Amelia Randall had to rasp angry words and glower at her morose husband before he aligned himself with the men who ob-

viously comprised the ruling body of Santa
Luiz.

"Mornin' to you, Chief Ahone," Frazier
greeted without enthusiasm, as Edge lit his cigarette and noticed that the brave to whom he
had surrendered was not on the plaza. "Folks
here are real anxious to know you ain't blamin'
any of us for the killin' of the brave last evenin'."

The Apaches ranged in age from their early
twenties to their mid-forties and were well fed
and healthy looking, as if the Gallo Rancheria
were better run and supplied than most. Their
chief was among the oldest, his Indian hand-
someness matched by the solidity of his taller
than average frame. Had he been grinning, the
lack of a shirt from his city-style attire might
have appeared faintly ridiculous. But the stony
expression he wore as he shifted his dark-eyed
stare from Frazier to Edge and back again left
little room in anyone's mind for anything but
fearful reflection upon his intentions.

"Your people and mine have always been
friends, white eyes," Ahone said slowly, as he
dismounted smoothly, swinging a leg over the
neck of his pony and sliding off the bare back.
The brave who had ridden closest to him also
got to the ground and held the rope bridles of
both pinto animals. "It is my wish that this will
always be so."

"It was self-defense, Chief Ahone!" Frazier
came back quickly, triggering renewed tension
among the old-timers just as they were enjoying
relief at what the Apache had said. "Your brave
fired first from the bell tower and this man—"

"Joe Winchester was not one of my braves," the chief interrupted, turning his back on the group of old-timers to face Edge. "When Ahone on feet, you also stand," he said menacingly.

Edge nodded and rose from the bench. "No sweat. You outnumber me." He held up the cigarette. "It okay if I smoke?"

"If you got to, white eyes." He swung his head to look up at the bell tower, and then back to the side of the aspen grove where the impressions of wheel rims in the dust showed the night parking place of the drummer's wagon. "I was told what happened. That was a fine shot."

"I was told you wouldn't be here for a long time. That was some riding."

Ahone shook his head. "The braves did not have to bring their dead brother all the way to Rancheria, white eyes. It was learned many days ago the Apache killer was in these mountains. So we were camped close by."

"Apache killer?" DeHart rasped, and stared hard at the half-breed.

There were similar responses from many of the old-timers scattered around the plaza. Ahone's revelation also drew reactions from the majority of the Apaches, but their anger seemed to have no tangible target.

"Your friend has gone?" the chief asked.

Edge's fear had expanded for an interminable second, and after taking the cigarette from his lips, he went through the motions of scratching his cheek to mask the shaking of his hand. He had done his share of Indian fighting in the violent past, much of it down here in the Southwest and in Mexico, where the hostiles were invariably Apaches. But when Ahone asked about the German drummer, the half-breed realized there was a good chance that he himself was off the hook.

"He ain't a friend, feller. Just somebody I made give me a ride after he scared my horse into breaking a leg."

"That's right, Chief Ahone," Frazier put in anxiously. "It was plain there was no love lost between the drummer and Edge here."

"I want to hear from you, Phil Frazier. I ask you," the Apache leader said quietly, but with a cold menace that was emphasized by the fact that he did not turn to look at the man.

"Philip, take care!" the short and stout Mrs. Frazier called.

"He took off in the middle of the night." Edge supplied the information, aware of a new and deeper tension that was gripping the old-timers. He guessed that whatever degree of faith they had previously had in Ahone was totally negated by what they considered to be an uncharacteristic attitude toward the one-eyed Frazier. "Said how he was real anxious to be long gone before you and your braves reached town."

The city-suited Apache nodded as he shifted his cold eyes from the half-breed to the tracks in the dusty plaza of the wagon that had recently arrived and then left the way it had come.

"He has gone toward Thunderhead. The way back is guarded by a band of my braves. If the Apache killer had attempted to return, I would have known of it."

Edge dropped his half-smoked cigarette and ground it under a boot heel. "You sure you're on to the right feller?"

"Why should I have doubt, white eyes?"

"He didn't strike me as the Indian-fighting kind, feller. Just a fat little drummer with an itch for an easy dollar, peddling paint and perfume to ladies."

Ahone grimaced. "This is what Joe Winchester of the Mescalero tribe tells to my Tonto braves who are working here for the white eyes of Santa Luiz. That the Apache killer, he now sells to women. But a year ago, he has something else in his wagon. Whiskey which he sells to the stupid Mescaleros. Bad whiskey, white eyes. This many braves die of the poison he sells. And this many squaws. Even a child sick with the fever." The chief, speaking in a dull tones held up fingers to show that fifteen men and four women had been fatally poisoned by the rot-gut liquor.

"They were fools, but they were our brothers. And all Apache braves are sworn to avenge them. You will help us, white eyes."

Edge said nothing, simply cocked his head in a quizzical manner.

"As the Mescalero are brothers of the Tonto, so you and the people of Santa Luiz are one. You will hunt the Apache killer and bring him to me to suffer the punishment for what he has done."

The chief's comparison triggered a surge of anxious whispering among the old-timers. Ahone waited for this to subside, his dark eyes revealing just a slight sign of incomprehension at Edge's lack of reaction. "You will do this," he went on in a harsher tone, "because if you do not, I will kill every white eyes here."

This time the burst of talking was much louder than whispers. The Apache chief had unequivocally confirmed the suspicion his previous comment had aroused. Shock and some hysteria were vented in a rising crescendo that filled the plaza with a babble of sound, against which no protest could be heard clearly.

But the brave who was holding his own and Ahone's horse understood an order signaled by the chief, and he aimed his Spencer repeater skyward and exploded a shot into the hot, shimmering air. Silence descended, as an almost palpable, suffocating presence.

Ahone turned his back on Edge and swung his head from side to side to insure that all the elderly citizens of Santa Luiz could see the determination in his face.. The goatee-bearded Newman was stricken by a coughing fit, and the Apache chief waited patiently until it was over. Then:

"Okay," he said to Edge, but loud enough for all to hear. "We Tonto Apaches of the Gallo Rancheria have no wish for war with white eyes. But we will not crouch in our wickiups when there is chance to punish the one who killed many of our brothers. And if we must go on warpath to do this, so be it."

He pointed the index finger of a rock-steady hand at Edge. "Whether it be so, you shall decide. You will track the Apache killer, find him and bring him to this place. Alive, white eyes. On penalty of the lives of all these others of your kind." He folded the finger into the fist of his hand and shuffled his feet to do a complete turnaround, arm still extended to encompass the entire shocked population of Santa Luiz.

"Kill me now, if you've a mind," the morose Elmer Randall blurted. "But I'm gonna have my say, Ahone! Why you doin' this? Why the stranger? He ain't got no reason to care what happens to us."

The Apache chief was facing the half-breed again and did not glance over his shoulder at the complaining old-timer. "Is up to you, white eyes," he said bleakly. "Ahone speaks true when he says we do not want war. If it be known that just one Apache brave is hunting a white eyes, there will be much trouble. So you take much care. Unless what man with spiked beard speaks is true. For if these elders die, it will spark a fire which will burn for long in the whole of Apacheria. How much do you not care?"

"My guns are up on the ridge," Edge said.

"They will be where you left them."

"I don't have a horse."

Ahone issued an order in Apache and the dismounted brave brought both ponies forward and extended the reins of the chief's to the half-breed.

"You can ride without saddle?"

Edge took the reins and nodded in reply to the query.

"You have until the sun is at its highest in the sky tomorrow, white eyes. If the Apache killer is not brought to this place then, the massacre will begin."

Edge claimed the brave's pony and swung astride him. The brave without a mount climbed smoothly up to ride double behind another brave, as Ahone announced to the frightened throng of old-timers: "I say again, it is my wish that we will always be friends."

Then he gave a hand signal and the braves, who had remained silent and virtually immobile since reaching the plaza, wheeled their ponies and heeled them into movement. Some left the plaza the way they had arrived. Others veered away in different directions. Heading for concealment on the ridges around Santa Luiz, they would be able to look down upon the community from every angle and also keep watch on the terrain on all sides. Before the dust of their leaving had settled, Edge had fastened the canteen and saddlebag to his bedroll, draped the gear over the base of the pony's neck, and was astride him. The unshod hooves of his mount thudded on the plaza in the wake of the sounds receding up the surrounding slopes.

"Pay no mind to what my Elmer said, young man!" Amelia Randall called. "We trust you. And all our hopes and prayers go with you."

Many heads nodded in agreement, but hopelessness was expressed on most of the aged faces. The one-eyed Phil Frazier moved into the pony's path and struggled to keep his voice evenly pitched when he said: "We're all countin' on you, Mr. Edge. I beg of you not to let us down. Ain't many of us who ain't had the allotted span like it says in the Good Book. But the older folks get, the sweeter life is."

The half-breed touched the brim of his hat. "Obliged, feller."

Frazier's natural eye expressed puzzlement at Edge's words as the rider tugged on the reins to veer around him.

"For giving me something to look forward to."

Chapter Five

Just as Chief Ahone had promised, the half-breed's Winchester and Frontier Colt were still on the dusty ground where he had dropped them in the shadow of the rock outcrop. As he checked their loads, he sensed the presence of several braves nearby. But he could not see them.

He had ridden more than a mile southward over the parched terrain under the blistering sun before the sense of being watched ceased to cause an itch between his shoulder blades. But a few minutes later, as he rode along a pebble-littered stream bed that probably ran with water for only a few hours a year, he was conscious of being under surveillance again. He displayed no outward sign of his discovery and continued at the same pace, maintaining the same attitude as before. His slitted eyes checked the way ahead and casually moved to glance in other directions from time to time.

His easy riding posture astride the saddleless pinto pony gave no clue to his state of readiness to respond in the event of danger striking.

The water course angled across a gentle upward grade, and by the time he reached the crest, he had a bearing on his watcher—in front and to the right. He reined in the pony, stroked the animal's neck, and murmured softly at the pricked ears: "If it's the ghost of Joe Winchester, I got to hope he didn't learn to be a straight shooter in the happy hunting ground."

The way ahead now lay across a broad expanse of grotesquely eroded sandstone, where not even a blade of scrub grass grew; barren land cracked by ravines between jagged-topped walls of rock that were often sheer. A dead and dangerous piece of territory for man and animal, even if nature were the only enemy. Although it was only a few square miles in area, a rider could easily become lost in the maze of ravines and die before he found a way out, or the soft sandstone among the flanking ridges might crumble beneath a mount to plunge horse and rider to their deaths.

There would certainly be a way around the daunting expanse, but it would take several hours to negotiate. So the half-breed chose to press on due south, seeking to save time and thereby improve the chances of the threatened old-timers at Santa Luiz. A Southern course would also offer him more opportunities to find out who was accompanying him—and why.

He clucked the pony forward and headed down into a ravine that zigzagged far across the dead land in a series of dog-leg turns. Sometimes the ravine was just wide enough for a rider to pass along and sometimes fifty feet separated one rock face from the other, while its depth varied from twenty to maybe seventy-five feet. Down at the lowest stretches in the solid shade, it was hot as hell, as if the sheer walls held prisoner the heat of a thousand high summers.

Edge had to run the back of a hand constantly across his narrowed eyes to brush away the beads of sweat which trickled off his brow and threatened to sting the sensitive membranes and blur his vision. Often he spat the salty moisture that gained entry to his mouth through lips curled back in an eager grin.

By watching him from ahead in the manner of Joe Winchester, the pursuing Apache had in this terrain become the pursued. And although Edge was hungry to corner him, he was patient. There was no danger; if the brave meant him harm, he could have made his play a hundred times before now.

At an intersection perhaps a half-mile into the twisting and turning ravine, another ravine curved off out of sight to the right and dead-ended at a cave-in to the left. The way ahead was clear for two hundred feet before a sharp, upward turn. Edge halted the pony, dismounted and took a drink of Santa Luiz spring water. It tasted of heat and the taint of being in the canteen several hours. He allowed the pinto to drink a little from his cupped hand, then let the rope reins hang from the bridle to the ground. The well-schooled animal remained still at the center of the intersection of the ravines. He left all the gear, including the Winchester, draped upon the pony and swung to the left. Thirty feet in that direction and some ten feet up the debris of the ancient cave-in brought him to a spot where he could squat on his haunches, out of sight of where the pinto stood and able to keep watch on every approach to his hiding place.

He cocked his Colt and held it loosely in his right hand, hanging between his knees. With his left he continued to rub at the greasy sweat, which beaded on his smooth forehead and irritatingly trickled down through the bristles on his cheeks and jaw and throat. He started to smell the odor of his armpits, his crotch, and his feet. It was a stink that a hard country drifter like Edge was used to, and he endured it with the same brand of stoicism as he endured the discomfort of his position among the rocks.

Time slid into history while Edge kept his ears strained for the first sound that would indicate the Apache was coming to see what had happened to the white eyes. He would see the horse, and suspicion would win the battle with curiosity, which had undoubtedly been taking place in his mind since he realized Edge had stopped. And then he would probably become ultracautious. Certainly he would not make a direct approach to the quiet, abandoned horse. Edge had allowed for this likelihood by taking up a position from which he could cover every direction.

How long he squatted on the rugged rocks would have been difficult to guess had it not been for the movement of a line of shade as the sun swung across the sky. In the heat and the stillness, the passing of time could play tricks in a man's mind. Thirty minutes or so had passed, he estimated, when he heard the distinctive sound of an unshod horse, walking along the ravine from the south. Now the half-breed's eager grin broadened as he tipped backward onto his rump and then stretched out on his back.

The pony was heading for one of its own kind, and there was scant chance that an Apache brave was astride him. So, sprawled out on his back, Edge's slitted, glinting eyes raked the skyline of the ridges where they met at the intersection of the ravines, listening as intently as he watched and struggling to block the clopping sound of unshod hooves from his mind.

He heard a pebble rattle, fifteen feet above and to the left of him. His lips curled back farther from his gleaming teeth. He tracked the muzzle of the Colt and his eyes to the point where he knew the Apache was going to show himself. Then he abruptly became as unmoving as the rocks on which he lay, held his breath and felt the salty beads of sweat turn to ice on his face—his instinctive reaction to the terrifying sound of a rattlesnake, whose vibrating tail was no more than two feet away from his head.

For the second time this morning he saw the head, shoulders, and revolver-gripping fist of an Indian appear above a rock, standing in silhouette against the brilliance of the sky. At the same time he heard the rattler's belly make dry slithering sounds on the rocks, but the sound of its anger had diminished. Yet, without being able to see the snake—the brim of his Stetson

67

blocked his view—the half-breed was certain the creature had turned to bring its exploring tongue and deadly fangs closer to his head.

The Apache brought his other hand into sight and moved it in front of his face. Just before sweat rolled into his eyes to reduce the clarity of his vision, Edge saw that one of the Indian's fingers was extended and pressed to his lips in a gesture that was a command to silence. The half-breed thought, but did not say: *I ain't about to whistle the "Battle Hymn of the Republic," feller*.

The rattler's head came into view on the very periphery of his vision. It was a diamond-back, yellow and black, and with a beady eye that surveyed Edge's unmoving profile with apparent disinterest, while its tongue flicked constantly as if to taste the air. Its fangs gleamed more sharply than the teeth of its potential victim, and the rattle in its tail ceased to sound until a shadow fell across its head—the shadow of a hand clutching a revolver. The shadow also fell across Edge's cheek as the diamond-back raised and swung its head to strike.

The gunshot seemed to the ears of the half-breed to have the power of a twenty-pounder cannon. The fangs ceased to gleam, and a liquid warmer and stickier than sweat splashed across Edge's face. Both ponies snorted in response to the shot and its echoes along the ravines.

Edge let the stale air trapped in his lungs rasp out in a noisy sigh through his clenched teeth, then used the back of his free hand to wipe the sweat from his eyes and the blood and pieces of snake flesh off his cheek.

"Hey, white eyes! Can now see why some of us Indians call you people pale faces!" The brave, who had stood to his full height on the top of the rock face, vented a harsh laugh.

Edge, feeling like he was drawing on a final reserve of strength, folded up into a sitting position. He glanced at the almost headless snake and muttered: "Long time since I been so rattled."

"What you say, white eyes?"

Now that the terror was diminishing, Edge recognized the voice of the same brave who had gotten the drop on him at the rock outcrop above Santa Luiz. "Whatever it was, it was out of order, feller," he growled, and tilted his head to look up at the Apache. "First thing I got to do is say much obliged." He holstered his Colt and hauled himself to his feet.

"Just doing the task my father set me," the brave answered, putting away his own gun. Before he started along the ridge to where he could make his way down into the ravine over the cave-in, he added: "He said to make sure you carry out the task he set you."

"One I owe you," Edge acknowledged, as he started down to where the two ponies were calm again in the wake of the gunshot.

The Indian paused on his journey to the same end. He drew a knife, and with a single powerful slashing action, severed the rattle off the tail of the diamond-back. He stowed it in a pouch on his belt and grinned as he patted the bulge. "Agent at Gallo pays well for these. Think he gets much more from stupid white eyes in the city."

"The cities don't have all the stupid white eyes," Edge answered.

The brave, who was in his mid-twenties, short but with a powerful build, wiped the grin from his craggily handsome face and became as impassive as the half-breed. "You pretty stupid to try to trick Poco Oso. But the snake, he was lucky for me. Make it easy. You planned to kill me?"

"If you'd aimed that old Colt at me, feller. Hardly ever allow a man to point a gun at me twice. Just needed to know who was watching me and why."

The Apache nodded and matched Edge's action of swinging astride his bay pony. "Now you do know, white eyes. Poco Oso, only son of Chief Ahone. Who, like his father, does not trust anyone he does not know. Red or white. And now this is known, we ride together?"

Edge was rolling a cigarette. He finished licking the paper and spat a shred of tobacco off his upper lip. "Makes sense, I guess."

"That is good. What is your name, white eyes?"

The half-breed lit the cigarette, and then both men heeled their ponies forward. "Edge."

Poco Oso vented his short laugh. "You pretty sharp one. To know tracker good as me is watching you."

"You ain't bad," Edge allowed.

After an easy silence of several minutes while they rode along the ravine, the Apache said: "I think you are a white who does not hate Indians only because they are Indians."

"Just."

"What you mean?"

"What *you* mean, feller. You mean *just* because, not *only* because."

The brave's handsome face showed a frown. "My American, it is not so good as I would like."

Edge spat sweat off his lips. "Hell of a lot better than my Apache."

There was another pause in the talk, until Poco Oso said suddenly: "I think we get along, Edge. Even if I am son of Chief Ahone, who forces you to hunt one of your own kind."

"We're all of a kind, feller. Under the skin." He bared his teeth in a cold grin. "Do things differently is all. Say this about you. You got a habit of coming over the tops of rocks. Not crawling out from under them."

The brave's grin had some warmth in it. "So Poco Oso, son of Chief Ahone, and the white eyes Edge can be friends?"

The half-breed's expression was briefly marred by a grimace of anger, as he recalled the vivid image of the tense scene before the bench by the aspen grove, when Ahone was making his demands.

Then his countenance became impassive as he growled: "I stood for your pa, feller. Figure for a while I can stand you."

Chapter Six

It took two hours to ride the rest of the way through the ravines, then the better part of another hour along a curving canyon to reach Thunderhead. So much for Amelia Randall's claim that the cross-country route from Santa Luiz was shorter than the route over the trails. It was only shorter for crows.

There was little talk between Poco Oso and Edge, and what they did say to each other was confined to a disjointed résumé by the Indian, of the crime of the Fritz von Scheel, and grunted or terse acknowledgments by the half-breed. The closer they drew to their objective, the less the Apache volunteered, withdrawing into a taciturn shell and offering no explanation for this mask of impassivity.

When he first became aware of the change in the brave, Edge thought he was merely tense at the prospect of finding the German in town. But by the time the buildings of Thunderhead began to take shape in the shimmering haze of noon, the half-breed had changed his opinion.

Poco Oso was one scared Apache.

"The whites in this place ain't so unprejudiced as me, uh?"

"What you mean?" The Indian continued to gaze fixedly at the buildings clustered in a fold between two low rises, about a mile southwest of the mouth of the curved canyon.

"Apaches are Apaches and they don't like them?"

"I have heard stories," the Indian answered. "But words do not frighten me." Having said this, he gave every appearance of conquering his fear. Certainly there was sincerity in his tone and expression when he looked at Edge to add: "I will come into the settlement of the white eyes with you. But it is important you know this is to help you in the task my father demands of you. Not because I do not trust you to do it."

"Suit yourself," the half-breed told him as they angled their ponies onto the trail, a few yards away from the crudely made and lettered sign that proclaimed the name of the community.

The rough-hewn marker with its faded lettering was in keeping with the unimposing town. The single street curved on an upgrade between two barren hills at the base of a much higher and steeper incline, which formed the outline of an arrowhead pointed to the south. That it was a mining town could be seen from the many claims which had been staked on the rugged slopes in back of Thunderhead. There were holes laboriously sunk into the rocky ground all over the slopes. Some miners had crude shacks nearby, others lived in tents, and a few resided in derelict covered wagons. There were gallows frames, sluices, and rockers on a few of the claims, on others just shovels and forks, and pails and pans. Much of the equipment was now discarded, left to rot on the sun-baked mountainside. Less than a quarter of the more than a hundred claims were still being worked, the smoke from cooking fires providing a ready reference to those shafts owned by miners who were still hitting pay dirt.

Because of a downdraft caused by the formation of the high ground, this smoke drifted across the slopes and merged with that from the chimneys of many of the buildings that flanked the fifty-foot-wide street to form an acrid-tasting, eye-stinging haze. There were no sidewalks on the street and just a few of the buildings, which rose like steps up its sloping curve, had stoops. Like the claims, which had been the sole reason for the existence of the town of Thunderhead, some of the single-story, timber, or adobe-built business premises had been abandoned. Opened doors and smoking chimneys distinguished those which were occupied from those which were not.

Few owners took the time and trouble to combat the ravages of the elements that patiently and relentlessly took their toll on anything man-made in country such as this. Paint was peeled or bubbled. Cracked windows went unrepaired and broken ones were fixed with boarding. Roof eaves sagged and shingles were askew. Metal was rusted and timber warped. Dust was piled like drifted snow wherever the wind had driven it. Bottles, cans, cartons, crates, paper, old clothing, building materials, and leftover food littered the street and the areas between the buildings.

"They are like the beasts of the fields, depositing their waste wherever it pleases them," the Apache muttered, as they started up the street, which as far as they could see was deserted.

"It ain't bullshit you're talking, feller," Edge growled.

The drugstore and the bakery were still in business on this lower end of the street. A loan agency and a fruit store were not. A man named Macdonald, who was a carpenter, no longer worked in a small adobe building once shared with a printer who had also left town. A bank across from a shuttered paint store was still in operation. A tailor had left Thunderhead, as had an attorney at law named Baldwin, a dentist called Overbay, one Joseph Wilde—who claimed to be the best photographer in the West—and a Miss Carter, music teacher. All had made their livings from tiny timber shacks which were little more than booths.

From the center of the curve to where the street simply petered out and became a track at the base of steeper ground where many spurs branched off toward the claims, there were fewer failed businesses. The signs were painted along the fronts of buildings or on shingles jutting out over doorways in a mixture of colors and a variety of lettering styles that were as untidy and ugly as everything else about Thunderhead. The smells of cooking, burning tabacco, horses, stale liquor, sweat, and other human waste matter almost masked the taint of wood smoke in this section of town.

A dog sprawled on its side in the hot shade below the stoop roof of the Fresh Meat Market was the only living thing the newcomers had seen since reaching town. But both were aware of watching eyes, many pairs of them, observing their progress with hostility. The only sound which reached out into the street from any of the buildings emanated from an out-of-tune piano, playing a mournful melody behind the frosted glass windows of the dance hall.

The only building in this area of town that was obviously abandoned, its window empty of glass, its door off its hinges, and its roof partially collapsed, was the jail and law office. Several bullet holes in the façade and areas of fire scorching around the window and doorway indicated that there had been violent trouble before Thunderhead lost its lawman.

"Need something with more taste than water to lay the trail dust in my throat," Edge said, as he tugged on the reins to head for the hitching rail out front of the Mother Lode Saloon.

"I will wait outside with the horses," Poco Oso answered, continuing to look around suspiciously.

"Ain't you thirsty, feller?" The both of them dismounted and hitched the reins to the rail.

"From the stories I hear, my kind can do the bad work in this town. But they not allowed in the white eyes' places."

"A man can never be sure of anything until

he's tried it for himself," Edge growled. "But stay thirsty if you want." He turned his back on the Apache, who was obviously of two minds and awhile away from reaching a decision, and pushed through the batwings which opened directly into the saloon off the street.

The place was deeper than it was wide, with a fifty-foot-long bar running down the left-hand side, sawdust on the floor in front of the bar, a dozen and a half chair-ringed tables, and half as many spittoons. The ceiling was hung with kerosene lamps, the walls were of natural-colored adobe, and the timber roof was unpainted. Four large mirrors with glass- and bottle-lined shelves in front of them covered the back wall of the bar. The furniture was solid and of good quality, but time and uncaring customers had mistreated it.

The Mother Lode smelled like every saloon Edge had ever been in. And it would have been easy to think that he had seen the two bartenders and ten customers many times before. The two leather-aproned men behind the counter were in their fifties and as much alike to be brothers: tall, broad, and fat-bellied. Their black hair was receding and their mean-eyed, wan, and heavily jowled faces were unshaven.

A quartet of their customers were seated at a table, playing cards and pretending to show no interest in the newcomer. They were also in their fifties and were cleanly dressed, freshly shaved that morning, and with soft hands: storekeepers or clerks. Three tougher and younger looking men sat at a nearby table, sharing a bottle of rye and making no attempt to hide their

78

curiosity about the half-breed. Like the beer-drinking card players, they carried no guns—at least none that showed. They were miners, maybe.

A tall, thin man with the complexion of a old boozer was leaning on the counter at the very back of the saloon. He was at least seventy and wore a suit that was too large for him and a Stetson that was too small. He was concerned only with the half-empty glass of flat beer in front of him, perhaps trying to determine whether he would fall over should he raise an elbow from the bartop to drink it.

The remaining two customers also stood at the bar. They were in their forties, tall and broad and muscular. Dressed in work clothes and with knives in sheaths hung on their belts, the dirt of many years hard work was ingrained into the pores of their flesh. Maybe a week had passed since they had shaved. More men off the claims, perhaps, drinking beer and watching Edge in one of the mirrors.

"How are you, stranger? What can I get you?" The bartender, who had a wart on the point of his jaw, greeted Edge, unsmiling.

"Dry, and a beer to ease that," the half-breed answered.

"You like Apaches, mister?" This from the slightly taller, redheaded man at the bar, who was five feet away and closest to where Edge stood.

"Don't stir the shit, Earl," the bartender growled, as he drew the beer and set it down in front of his new customer.

"Earl just asked a plain and simple question,

79

Jordan," the other man at the bar put in. He had been hurt in a knife fight. The scar was livid and puckered, running three inches across his left cheek.

"And the stranger ain't givin' me no answer, Jesse," Earl complained, in the same dull tone as before.

Edge continued to drink his beer, allowing the cool liquid to run slowly down his dusty throat.

"And you two ain't bought but the one shot each since you come in. Hour ago." Jordan put the half-breed's money in a pocket of his apron and exchanged a sour look with the other bartender.

Edge emptied his glass, set it down, and said to Jordan: "Took care of my dryness, feller. Like a drink now. Rye."

"Don't reckon you're hard of hearin', mister," Earl said.

Edge allowed his eyes to meet the other man's in the mirror. "You talking to me?"

"I seed you ride in. On an Apache pony. Along with an Apache on an Apache pony."

"You know I ain't deaf, and now I know you ain't blind, feller," Edge answered, paying for the drink Jordan had poured. "Anything else we should know about each other before we go our separate ways?"

"Sassy sonofabitch, ain't he, Earl?" Jesse growled.

"Take care you guys," one of the miners at the table warned, sounding a little nervous. "He packs a gun and looks like the kind of guy knows how to use it."

"I saw that," Jordan put in quickly. "And I told them not to stir the shit, didn't I?"

The card game came to a sudden end, and chair legs scraped on the floor. Beer was hurriedly tossed against the backs of throats.

"Afternoon, Jordan. George."

The other three storekeepers or clerks muttered their good-byes, and then all four hustled out of the saloon.

"Great, ain't it, George?" Jordon snarled. "They ain't drinkin' themselves and now they stir the shit to drive out the customers that are."

"If you ain't deaf, you heard my question, mister?"

Edge threw the rye down his throat, relished the glow it left in its passage, and asked: "Did they hang your pa for horse stealing and was your ma a buck-and-a-half whore in Virginia City?"

"Son of a friggin' bitch." Jesse spoke the words very clearly.

The piano played softly in the distance, the music still mournful. Then the batwings flapped. Footfalls sounded softly on the sawdusted floor. Edge saw rage spread across the reflected face of Earl in the mirror, then glimpsed an image of Poco Oso coming toward him.

"Oh, this is gonna do it," Jesse added.

"Get that stinkin' Indian out of this place!" Earl roared, whirling away from the bar.

Edge did not fall into the trap of the distraction, but kept his narrowed eyes fixed upon Earl, first in the mirror, then in the flesh. He was aware of the knife being drawn from the

81

sheath before he turned to face the big man and had the Frontier Colt drawn and cocked by the time Earl lunged toward him, left hand reaching to grab the front of Edge's shirt and right fisted around the knife handle for an upward thrust at the crotch. The brown-skinned hand, wrapped around the butt of the revolver, moved only fractionally. The trigger finger squeezed.

Gasps of shock accompanied the gunshot. Earl halted and dropped both arms to his side, looking down at his big boots. There was a hole neatly drilled in the cap of the left one, and blood oozed up out of it, darkening in hue as it was absorbed by dust. "I don't friggin' believe it," he croaked. He leaned heavily against the bar counter, weakened by shock rather than pain.

Edge tracked the Colt slightly to the side, thumbed back the hammer, and squeezed the trigger a second time.

Earl groaned and swung to face the counter, holding on to it with both hands—one of them still fisted around the knife. His stance was twisted and awkward because his feet, both now bleeding, did not move.

"Once maybe," Edge said evenly. "But there ain't no denying twice, I figure."

"Jesus!" one of the seated miners hissed.

Earl started to slide down the front of the bar. But Jesse stepped quickly forward and supported him with a thick arm across his shoulder blades, hand under an armpit. His scarred face expressed horror and revulsion as he stared at

82

the half-breed over his partner's sagging head.

"You gotta be the meanest sonofabitch I ever did lay eyes on, mister," he tried to snarl. But he sounded only husky.

"Figure you ain't been around much."

"Damnit, I'm startin' to hurt, Jesse," Earl growled. "Get me to a chair, why don't you."

"Sure, old buddy."

Jesse exhibited his obvious strength by lifting Earl with a smooth ease, carrying him to a chair vacated by one of the storekeepers, and lowering him into it.

Edge extracted the spent shell cases from his Colt and reloaded the gun, while he watched the three miners at the table recover from their shock and start to stoke their anger.

"Mister," Jordan said.

"Yeah?"

"You're a stranger hereabouts and it don't appear Earl and you know each other from some other place."

"I don't have to know a man to shoot him, feller."

"But how'd you know the way to rile Earl the way you did? How'd you know his ma and pa back on the farm in Pennsylvania are the only folks he gives anythin' close to a damn about?"

"Didn't. Used them to make a point. What he thinks of his folks is the same as my opinion of Apaches. Our own business." He holstered the Colt, glanced to where the brave had been standing—midway between the batwings and the bar—since Earl had launched his ill-fated attack, and asked: "What's your poison, feller?"

"I like whiskey," Poco Oso answered, his readiness to meet more trouble far more obvious than the tension within Edge.

"Then you buy it someplace else, redskin!" Jordan growled.

"Attaboy!" Earl snarled through teeth clenched in an evil grin.

"He ain't buying," Edge said, and placed a dollar bill on the bartop beside his empty glass. "I am. Owe him."

Jesse moved away from the chair in which the helpless Earl sat with the blood starting to congeal on the toe caps of his boots. Chair legs scraped on the floor, one of the chairs tipping over backward, as the three men who had been seated at the next table got to their feet. George moved up alongside Jordan. Each man wore an expression of depthless hatred for the Apache brave, and in his stance was an unshakable determination to uphold the racist rule of the house.

Earl continued with his evil grin, anticipating revenge for his treatment by Edge. The old-timer with the ill-fitting clothes who had shown only a mild interest in external events after the two shots, was back contemplating his flat beer.

"I like it but I can do without, Edge," Poco Oso said, tense but not afraid. "We waste time anyway. Apache killer is not here."

"You're wrong, Injun!" Jesse snarled. "We all done our share of wastin' savages like you!"

"Not me," the old man at the far end of the bar said. And his contribution surprised everybody, drawing most eyes toward him. He continued to gaze into his beer. "Though it ain't my fault I ain't had that pleasure. Just never got to be in the right place at the right time. Had cause, God knows. Personally, I don't reckon a 'Pache is worth the waste of water to spit on."

"Well, I'll be," George said with a shake of his head. "Don't reckon I ever heard old Tom say that many words all at once before."

"Give him a drink out of my dollar," Edge instructed, and drew all attention back to him again. "Seems I owe him, too."

"Aw, shit!" a miner rasped. This upon seeing that the half-breed had taken advantage of the distraction to slide the Colt out of his holster again and was resting the butt on the bar, barrel aimed at Jordan's midsection.

"Frig it, he won't kill you!" Earl snarled. He snapped his head from side to side to look with blazing eyes at Jesse and the other three miners. "Go get him and beat the shit outta him!"

Edge, eyes narrowed to threads of glinting ice blue and lips pulled back to display only the dark lines between his upper and lower teeth, thumbed back the hammer of the Frontier Colt. He could see the fear of the two bartenders directly, the reflection of the miners' indecision in a mirror, and could hear the Apache breathing fast behind him.

"I wouldn't bet on that, Earl!" Jordan said huskily, and snatched a bottle off the shelf. "I got this guy's measure."

He slid the bottle along the counter top. Edge stopped it with his free hand, raised it, and pulled the cork with his teeth. He spat out the cork and set down the bottle.

"That was smart, Jordan," he said evenly, his lips curled back farther now to display a cold grin. "To figure out I'm a feller who'll go to any lengths to get what I want. With Earl just a couple of bad feet. You just kept yourself away from a graveyard." He eased the bottle along the bartop. "Take a drink."

The Colt had never wavered in its aim, and the anger and hatred on the faces of the men had a frozen quality. Then some of them made strangled sounds of frustration deep in their throats, as Poco Oso raised the bottle and sucked down a slug.

"Is enough, Edge. You have made another point. We go look for Apache killer now."

The half-breed took the bottle and slid it back along the bar. Jordan and George both let it pass. Old Tom caught it.

"You ain't gonna drink that?" Earl snarled. "After an Apache sucked on it?"

"Ain't nothin' better than rye whiskey to kill all kinda germs," the old man answered, pouring liquor in with his stale beer.

"Figure if any of you fellers saw a drummer called von Scheel come to town, you wouldn't be ready to tell me?" Edge asked, as he began to back toward the batwings, Colt leveled at no one in particular now. The Apache moved beside him, but watched the doorway and sunny street beyond.

Of the Thunderhead men, only Jordan moved—along the bar to pick up the dollar bill Edge had left. He tore it in two, placed the halves together, and tore them again. Then he allowed the shreds to float to the floor. "Means

86

I still ain't sold no liquor for a stinkin' Apache to drink," he snarled, as a bead of sweat dripped off the wart on his jaw.

"I best get Doc Riordan to fix up your feet, Earl," Jesse said hoarsely.

"Frig it, I don't want any help from any of you yellow sonsofbitches!" the wounded man snapped. He tried to haul himself out of the chair but yelled in pain and fell hard to the sawdusted floor.

Poco Oso stepped out through the batwings and held them open for Edge to leave the Mother Lode, sliding the revolver back into its holster.

A tall, gaunt man, who was leaning a hip against the hitching rail and smoking a long cheroot, said, "Them guys in there weren't packin' guns, mister."

His arms were hanging loosely at his sides, and he did not move them, merely inclined his head a little to direct a glance down at the pearl-handled Remington .44 in the holster that was tied at the toe to his left thigh.

Edge turned slowly to look at the man, who was dressed entirely in black—which served to emphasize the glints of metal from the bullets in the slots of his gunbelt and the star-in-a-circle badge of the territorial marshal pinned to his left shirt pocket. "I see it, feller. Should it bother me?"

"Only if your business with von Scheel conflicts with my interest in him."

The Apache whistled softly through pursed lips.

"What do you have in mind for him, feller?"

"Take him back to Los Alamos so the folks there can see him hang." He was able to spit without taking the cheroot from the corner of his mouth. "And ain't nothin' anybody can do that'll make a jot of difference to what I have in mind, mister."

Edge nodded. "Then, Marshal, it seems we could have an explosive situation."

Chapter Seven

Now Poco Oso grunted, and there was anger in the sound.

"What's with the Indian?" the marshal asked.

"While he's making noises at you, he ain't trying to kill you."

The lawman smiled, and there was both humor and eagerness in the expression. "He can try."

The scar-faced Jesse pushed out through one of the batwing doors, so as not to bang Edge in the back. He shared a scowl among the Apache, the half-breed, and the marshal. "Lot of friggin' use havin' the law in Thunderhead again! When a fast-draw gunslinger can walk into a peaceable saloon and shoot up an innocent citizen. Then stand out on the street chewin' the damn fat with the guy with the badge!"

"Look of the law office, it figures this town got no use for a man with a badge," the marshal answered.

Jesse spat, and the dusty, sun-baked surface of the street absorbed his saliva as thirstily as it had the lawman's. Then he strode angrily away from the saloon, angling toward a small frame building at the center of a block comprised of the law office, a clothing store, kerosene suppliers, and pawnbrokers.

"We talk to him, Edge," the Apache said.

"You willing to listen?" the half-breed asked the lawman.

"I got a coffepot on the stove. Name's Larsen. Known in the Santa Fe area for my hospitality. And my stubborn streak."

He swung away from the rail and started across the street, heading for the bullet-riddled and fire-ravaged law office. Edge and the Apache trailed him. As they entered through the drunkenly hanging door, a man emerged from the building into which Jesse had gone. A red-faced, fat man of middle years, with the crumbs of what he was eating for lunch lodged in his gray moustache and a napkin still tucked in his shirt collar. He carried a black doctor's bag.

"Herr Edge, you come to help me, *bitte*?"

The half-breed, who was ahead of Poco Oso as they entered the law office, heard something akin to hope in von Scheel's voice. But it soon turned to despair when he added: "*Mein Gott*, an Apache Indian!"

There was nothing left of the office's furnishings but a desk and a stove, and there was no furniture at all in the two cells, their rows of bars fitted with two doors and another row of bars at right angles in the center. Upon seeing the brave, the drummer backed away from the bars to press himself against the angle of two walls. His clothing was now rumpled and streaked with dirt, while his face was sprouting black and gray bristles. His small green eyes were red-rimmed from lack of sleep and deep anxiety.

"No, feller. Come to decide whether you hang or die Apache style."

"Help yourself," Larsen invited, as he rested his rump on the side of the desk. "But only to coffee."

The lawman was a match for the half-breed's six feet three inches but his build was a lot slighter, and he was a couple of years older. His eyes were coal black, set in deep sockets above prominent cheekbones. His neatly cut hair and thin moustache were as black as his Stetson, kerchief, shirt, gunbelt, pants, and boots. But his teeth were yellow. His saddle and bedroll, which were piled in the angle of the rear wall, and the bars of the empty cell were also black. "You want to come on in?" he asked of Poco Oso, as Edge took the coffeepot off the stove and brought it to the desk. The half-breed emptied the dregs from one of the two tin cups onto the floor and refilled it.

"I okay here," the brave said from the doorway, without shifting his unblinking gaze from the man behind the bars.

"It wasn't just a suggestion," Larsen rasped, draping his left hand over his gun butt. "Like for you two to be close so neither can jump me."

"Inside and have some coffee," Edge drawled, holding up the pot.

Poco Oso stepped over the threshold but shook his head as he went to lean against a wall directly opposite to the frightened prisoner in the cell. "I have all I need."

Larsen eyed Edge balefully. "Your buddy hasn't got my message yet. He's mine." The lawman never took the cheroot from his mouth.

Von Scheel nodded vigorously. "That is right, Herr Larsen. I am your prisoner. You have responsibility for me."

"Shut your damn mouth," the marshal instructed evenly, without shifting his attention away from Edge, who had replaced the coffee-pot on the stove and now went to sit down on the floor, leaning his back against the wall a few feet from where the Apache stood. "How'd he get your buddy so hot under the collar for his hide?"

"You want to tell about that?" the half-breed asked of the brave, and took grateful sips of the strong coffee while, in a monotone, Poco Oso spoke of how the Mescalero men, women, and child had died as a result of drinking whiskey sold to them by the German drummer.

"I sell in good faith!" von Scheel blurted as soon as the Apache was finished. "There vas no means for me to tell the vhiskey vas bad. Vhen I hear vhat has happened, I throw avay all I have left! I svear this!"

Larsen merely turned his head to gaze coldly through the bars at the German, thereby bringing the prisoner's plea to an end. "Somethin' you and your buddy should know, Edge." His cheroot was now a stub, and he took a fresh one from a case in a shirt pocket and lit it from the end of the first. "I got no love for the Apaches. But long as they don't step out of line, I got no feelin's against them. Like them fellers you had a run-in with across at the saloon."

"Poco Oso has just told you the half of it, Marshal," Edge said.

Larsen held up a hand. "Hear me out, mister. This animal I got behind the bars here ain't no average, run-of-the-mill job to me. See, Los Alamos is my home town. And I know the family he killed. Everyone knows everyone else in Los Alamos."

It was very hot in the law office, both from the heat of the day and the stove, and also very quiet. The piano player had stopped his music after the two shots were fired in the saloon, but now he started again. The only sound that drifted in from outside was his music, and its melody was as melancholy as it had been at the start. It suited Larsen's tone of voice and the expression on his gaunt face.

"A month ago it happened. I work out of Santa Fe, so I wasn't there. But I heard about it. This guy rolls into town with his wagonload of sweet-smellin' junk for the ladies. And makes his pitch to Mr. and Mrs. Hart, who run the Los Alamos Drugstore. They were gonna buy some of the stuff, but there wasn't enough in the cash drawer. So Clayton Hart, he went out back to the parlor to get the money from his hidey-hole. The drummer saw him and pulled a gun. He wanted it all. But it was the Harts' life savin's, and they was just a few weeks away from retirin'."

Larsen did his trick of spitting from one side of his mouth with the cheroot still held in the other. "Clayton had an old Dragoon Colt in with the money, and he tried to turn the tables on the drummer. I checked the gun. Mechanism locked solid with rust. That was when I got there a couple of days after the killin's, of course. The animal behind the bars here, he shot Clayton in the head. Then Clayton's old lady in the heart. Miss Emily Jane, their spinster daughter, who happened to be passin' at the time, she got a bullet in the belly and lived long enough to tell how it was. Tell, too, how her folks had eight hundred and fifty-six dollars and thirty-five cents saved."

The lawman raised his rump off the desk, emptied the dregs of the spare coffee cup and took it to the stove to fill with fresh coffee. "Oh, somethin' else," he went on with a brief, contemptuous glance at von Scheel, who was still pressed into a corner of his cell. "The old folks was both blind."

Now he looked at Edge and the Apache for a reaction to the punch line of his account. Poco Oso continued to stare levelly across the office and into the cell. Edge said:

"Can understand why their neighbors are so anxious to have you bring him in, Marshal."

"Damn right, mister!" he snapped, a hint of anger in his voice. "I never did get on his trail. I just took off and asked every place I came to if a foreign guy of his description had been

94

around. Never did get a line on him. Just got lucky here in Thunderhead. Was bedded down in this place and heard a wagon rollin' up the street. Looked out and there he was. Large as life. Put the arm on him and locked him in the cell. Just waitin' now for the blacksmith to put new shoes on my horse. Then startin' back with him."

There was a look of challenge in his eyes and in the set of his jaw, as he again waited for a response from the half-breed and the Apache.

"You got time to listen to the half of our side the Indian didn't tell you?" Edge asked, as he rose to his feet, took off his hat, ran a shirt sleeve over his sweaty brow, and replaced the hat.

"You listened real well to me, mister."

"There's an old mission three or four miles north of here. Taken over by a bunch of sick old-timers who figure the mountain air and the spring water in the church is good for what ails them."

"Santa Luiz," Larsen said with a nod. "I've heard of it. Some of the folks there passed through Santa Fe on their way."

"But you never got to know them like the folks who live in Los Alamos, uh?"

"Just tell it, Edge."

"It isn't so healthy in Santa Luiz right now. On account of the thirty or so Apaches who are in the hills encircling the place. Scaring the hell out of the old folks. Because the Indians told them that if I don't deliver von Scheel to Santa Luiz before noon tomorrow, they're going to kill them."

The cheroot bobbed up and down at the side of Larsen's mouth, and for a second he closed his eyes, mouthing a curse.

"It is bad what the Apache killer did to the people in your town," Poco Oso said—this the first indication that he had heard and taken note of what was happening while he stared fixedly at the prisoner. "You and your people, it is right to want vengeance. But you give this man to Edge and me. And my father, Chief Ahone, will make him suffer greater punishment than white eyes' justice."

"You cannot do that!" von Scheel shrieked, launching himself across the tiny cell and making fists around the bars, the flesh of his face pale and trembling. "You cannot hand me over to the Apache Indians."

"God, what a situation," Larsen growled.

"I vould rather you shoot me down here in the cell in cold blood!" the German wailed.

The gaunt-faced marshal was obviously not a man used to suffering from indecision, and he unburdened himself of doubt very quickly on this occasion. His expression again toughened up, and his tone became the usual even drawl. "Shut your damn mouth," he told von Scheel. Then to Edge: "I'll go check on my horse, mister. We'll leave soon as he's shod."

"For Santa Luiz?" the Apache asked.

The German began to speak in his own language, in the cadences of a prayer.

"I'm a lawman. If innocent people are in danger, it's my sworn duty to try to protect them."

"You're an asshole is what you are! For even

96

thinkin' for a lousy second about handin' over a white to the stinkin' Apaches!"

The four men in the law office snapped their heads around to look at a fifth, a man who had seemed to fold himself off the front wall of the building to stand splay-legged in the doorway. He was aiming a double-barrel shotgun from the hip.

Both Edge and Larsen reached instinctively for their holstered revolvers.

"Pull them and everybody'll be just some sticky red stuff on the walls!" This was spoken by one of the two men who suddenly came up from crouches outside the glassless window. The speaker was Jordan, one of the bartenders from the Mother Lode, and he too aimed a shotgun—from the shoulder.

His look-alike, George, had a revolver in each hand, and he rested the barrels on the window-sill. "Best get your hands up high," he said. "Injun, on your feet."

The half-breed, the marshal, and the Apache complied with the instructions, while von Scheel said excitedly: "You are going to free me?"

The man on the threshold, whom Edge had not seen before, growled: "The stinkin' Apaches ain't the only ones know how to make a man die hard, you murderin' sonofabitch. And if you don't do like the marshal's been tellin' you and bide quiet, I'll prove it to you. Which would be a shame for the folks waitin' to see you swing."

The German sank to his knees, still gripping the bars. Tears of despair squeezed out of his flesh-thickened eyes, and his head fell forward, knocking off his hat. His body was racked by soundless sobs.

"Don't want to kill anyone here," the man in the doorway went on. "But able and willin' to if you men and the Indian don't ease out your guns real slow and toss them to me."

He was big, taller by a couple of inches than Edge and Larsen, solidly built from shoulders to hips, and dressed in sweat and dirt-stained work clothes that closely contoured his bulging muscles. He was about fifty years old, with a square jaw, thick moustache, and small eyes. His hair was gray and clipped to short as bristles. He gave a grunt of satisfaction and became less rigid in his stance when the three revolvers sailed across the office, came to rest at his feet, and three pairs of arms were again thrust into the hot air.

"What's with this, Hoy?" Larsen asked, as the town began to feed sounds into the law office: the voices of men, the snorts of horses, footfalls and hooves on the street, doors opening and closing, some laughter.

"Our business, mister. And when it's done, you can get on with your own. Right now, herd yourself into the other cell."

Edge was the first of the trio to comply with the order, his lean face betraying no clue to what he was thinking. Larsen mouthed a curse as he followed the half-breed's example. The Apache looked like he was determined not to do as he was told.

"He lied about you," Edge said to the Indian,

as he swung open the cell door and shot a glance at Poco Oso. "You he'd love to kill."

"Damn right."

The Apache, a silent snarl fixed on his face, joined the two white men in the cell. Hoy came into the law office, kicked the barred door closed, turned the key that was already in the lock and withdrew it. His shotgun had wavered a little when he held it in one hand, but the twin muzzles remained a constant threat.

"Thank Christ," George muttered.

Hoy opened a drawer of the desk, dropped the key inside, and closed the drawer, as Jordan and George withdrew from the window.

"You heard it all?" Larsen asked bitterly.

"Enough after I come down from the claim to find out what the shootin' was about. And Jesse Pardoe filled me in about the gunslinger and the Apache causin' trouble."

"You're goin' about this the wrong way, Hoy. You people are so full of hate for the Apaches you ain't takin' the time to think out how—"

"Didn't take much thinkin'," Hoy cut in, "after I heard about the Apaches bein' up at Santa Luiz ready to slaughter the old folks there. Knew right off what I was gonna do. Sent Jesse to tell folks to get ready and have the Woodin brothers bring their guns to give me a hand and put you men on ice. Then when I heard this here stinkin' Indian say he was the son of the chief . . . Well, shit, I don't see no way we can go wrong."

He went to the doorway and glanced out onto the street, where the dust raised by restless horses floated in the smoky haze. "Looks like we're about ready to leave," he told the prisoners. "Be back to turn you folks loose soon as it's done."

He swung out of the doorway, yelling for somebody to bring him his horse. One animal's hooves clopped on the surface of the sloping street. Then Hoy yelled: "Let's go get them, boys!"

It was impossible to tell how many horses were heeled into a gallop down the curving street. Some of the dust disturbed by the pounding hooves drifted into the law office and settled, before the sounds of the departing riders had faded from earshot.

Nobody was playing the piano anymore.

"Dammit to hell!" Larsen snarled, smashing his right fist into the palm of his left hand.

Von Scheel, who had curtailed his silent sobs after hearing Hoy's plan, laughed harshly as he awkwardly got to his feet. He picked up his hat and placed it on his head. "I am saved from the Apache Indians," he murmured gratefully. Now he was able to return the hatred in Poco Oso's gaze with a stare of triumphant defiance.

"Chief Ahone will care nothing that his son is a hostage of Apache-hating white eyes," the brave said coldly, interrupting his concentration on the German to share an intense look with Edge and Larsen. "There will be much blood spilled at the Mission of Santa Luiz so that he may live long enough to be hanged."

The marshal nodded, grimacing around his cheroot. "You don't have to tell me, Indian. I know Apaches well enough. And locked up in this jail, there ain't a damn thing we can do to stop a massacre at the mission." He eyed Edge balefully, as if he felt the half-breed was entirely to blame for what had happened.

"Something you want, feller?"

"Yeah, mister. I want outta here." He gripped the bars of the door and rattled them. "But when folks hit this place it wasn't hard enough. Cells are as secure as they ever were. Ain't no way out but through the friggin' door."

Edge had been rolling a cigarette. He pushed it into a corner of his mouth and said: "So I figure that's our only chance."

"Terrific!" Larsen snarled, as he whirled angrily to face the half-breed. "How we gonna do it? Kick the damn door down?"

Edge raised a hand, and Larsen rocked his head back, as if expecting to be hit. But the brown hand merely pulled the cheroot from his mouth to place its burning end to the cigarette. A gentle intake of breath from the glowing ash caused the fresh tobacco to puff smoke, and then Edge handed the cheroot back. "Obliged."

Larsen replaced the cheroot in his mouth and demanded: "Well, mister, you gonna answer me?"

"Seems to me," Edge said evenly, "that since you locked a prisoner in that other cell, you could have the key to our problem."

Chapter Eight

"Hot damn!" the lawman exclaimed and delved a hand into a pocket of his pants. "Why the hell didn't I remember that?"

"Because you worry too much about other people and not enough about yourself," the half-breed replied, as Larsen drew out a key.

"Your kind always puts number one first," the marshal growled, swinging toward the door and reaching through the bars to push the key into the lock.

Edge moved casually across the cell to the row of bars that divided it from von Scheel's. The German was close by on the other side, staring in horror as the black-clad lawman struggled to turn the key in the lock.

"In this number, feller, I'm the one the old-timers at the mission are relying on."

"Damn, it don't fit!" Larsen groaned.

Edge took a final half-stride forward and powered his right arm through the bars of the partition. A cry of alarm escaped the German as Edge fastened a grip on his fleshy left wrist. Then the hapless mass killer screamed in pain, as Edge wrenched him hard and fast against the bars.

"Figured it wouldn't," he said evenly, "seeing as how the key Hoy used to keep us here was already in the lock."

Von Scheel tried to pull away, but Edge forced the man's arm hard against the bars, threatening to snap it at the elbow. His pain showed itself in beads of sweat on his brow and in the way the veins stood out like blue cords at his temples and neck.

"What the hell, mister?" Larsen demanded.

"I vill shout for help," von Scheel rasped. "There vill be people left in this town to make sure ve do not escape."

Edge reached up his left hand as if to scratch his neck under the long black hair. But when it emerged it was fisted around the handle of the straight razor.

Von Scheel whispered something in German as the flat of the blade was positioned on the bulge of his cheek between two bars, the point no more than a quarter of an inch below a wide, green eye.

"You're nothing to nobody, here or anywhere else," the half-breed reminded him softly. "Except a corpse on the hoof. If you're ready for the slaughter now, start yelling. Or don't do what I'm going to tell you. I don't figure whoever comes running will love me any the less for seeing you with your brains trickling out of your eye socket."

"*Ja, ja,*" the fat drummer rasped. "I vill do vhat you say. You tell me."

"Edge, damnit, let us in on—"

"Out is what you said you wanted," the half-breed interrupted Larsen. "Reach through and unhook the lariat off your saddle."

The confused and angry lawman was slow to respond. But the Apache was quick to go down on his haunches and do the half breed's bidding.

"Fine," Edge said, and altered his grip on the German to take hold of the forearm. "Now tie an end around his wrist. Real tight. Not a slipknot."

Poco Oso obeyed, while von Scheel trembled and began again to mutter a prayer in his native language. Larsen, meanwhile, watched what was happening with a frown of puzzlement creasing his brow. The Apache wrenched hard on the rope to check that the knot was secure, and the German's plea to a higher authority was cut off by a groan of pain.

Edge grinned as he released his hold on the man and transferred it to the rope. "Reason I didn't have him tie it around your neck, feller." He replaced the razor in the neck pouch. "Larsen give him the key of his cell."

"What?"

Again the Apache responded quickly while the lawman was hampered by doubt. He reached out, plucked the key from Larsen's hand, and gave it to Edge, who pushed it through the bars, but kept hold of it when von Scheel gripped it.

"Here's what you're going to do," the half-breed said evenly. "Go to the door and open it. Walk across to the desk, get the key from the drawer, and bring it back here. Give it to me."

Edge let go of the key. It dropped from von Scheel's trembling, greasy fingers. "I'll make allowances for mistakes, feller. But if you try to do anything to queer this, you're good as dead. Pick up the key and start."

"I am good as dead vhatever I do," von Scheel said in despair.

"While there's life there's hope," the half-breed pointed out. "Poco Oso."

"Yes?"

"Show him your knife."

The Apache did so, drawing the weapon from the sheath on his weapon belt. Von Scheel swallowed hard.

"I'll just do the hauling back, feller. Then tie you to these bars. Facing us. Be up to the Apache Indian here to finish it then. And with no place to go, I guess he won't be in any hurry."

Edge had his back to Poco Oso, but the German could see the brave, and he nodded vigorously. "I vill do as you ask."

The half-breed gave the rope some slack, and von Scheel stooped to retrieve the key. Then he moved shakily across the cell to the door, where he reached between the bars with his untethered hand and inserted the key in the lock. It turned smoothly. He hesitated, leaning against the bars.

"The Indian is lookin' real eager for you to try somethin', mister!" Larsen warned.

The German groaned and used his free hand to wipe sweat from his face.

"Shut up, Marshal," Edge murmured, low-voiced but menacing. "He ain't no use to us passed out from fear."

Von Scheel swung open the door and stepped across the threshold, starting toward the desk after a brief yearning glance at the doorway and the bright street beyond. The only slack Edge allowed him was the natural sag of the lariat rope. When the German reached the desk, he looked back at the trio of men in the locked cell. There was now hatred showing through the fear on his fleshy face.

Poco Oso reached forward with the knife, running the flat of the blade rapidly across four bars and back again. Again terror, to the exclusion of all other emotions, asserted its hold on every line of von Scheel's face. Then, with a German curse, he yanked open the drawer, reached inside with his free hand, and came out with the key. But now he deviated from the instructions Edge had given him. Instead of returning the way he had gone, he came directly toward the door of the locked cell. He stopped short and held the key up for all to see.

"Come on, you bastard," Larsen urged grimly.

"I ask for your vord," the German said to Edge.

"Or what?" the half-breed countered.

"I vill throw the key out of the vindow and begin to scream for help. As you have said, I am nothing to the people here. But they vould not

107

allow me to suffer slow death by an Apache Indian." He ignored Larsen's harsh curse and continued to gaze at the impassive face of Edge. "So you make me promise, *mein herr*."

Edge nodded. "I'll kill you myself rather than hand you over to Ahone and his braves, feller."

Poco Oso, grunting his displeasure, again rattled his knife back and forth along the bars and drew the German's terrified green eyes to him. But the unfortunate mass killer soon returned his attention to the half-breed, reached a decision, and inserted the key in the lock. Then he backed off.

Larsen turned the key and swung open the door. "Loan me your knife, Indian," he said to the angered brave.

Poco Oso growled a single word in his native language.

"Do it, feller," Edge instructed, still gripping the rope. "This ain't the time or place to argue out our differences."

In a blur of speed, the Apache surrendered his knife, but ignored Larsen's outstretched hand to send the weapon spinning through the open doorway. The marshal cursed and threw himself against the wall. The blade sank an inch into the side of the desk, the handle quivering with the force of the impact.

There was contempt in the brave's voice when he said: "If I had wanted to kill you, white eyes lawman, you could not have moved fast enough."

"Sonofabitch!" Larsen snarled.

"Attend to your prisoner," Edge snapped.

The marshal did so. Going to the desk, he

withdrew the knife from the wood and cut the rope a foot short of where it was tied around öne of Von Scheel's wrists. Then, as Edge coiled the lariat, Larsen bound both wrists of the submissive German.

Poco Oso went out of the cell, reclaimed his knife, dropped to his hands and knees, and approached the glassless window. "Our ponies are gone," he reported.

Edge rehooked the lariat onto the saddle as he left the cell. "Where's the drummer's wagon and team?" he asked Larsen.

"Down at the livery stable."

"You see anybody watching this place, Poco Oso?"

"No. But that does not mean nobody is on guard."

Edge remained upright but hurriedly pressed himself against the wall at one side of the doorway. The revolvers that had been surrendered to Hoy still lay on the threshold where they had fallen. From his position Edge had a restricted view of one section of the broad street and a line of buildings on the far side: the Mother Lode Saloon, Canning's Dry-Goods Store, the barber shop, and Charlie's Livery Stables.

This area of Thunderhead looked as empty as it was silent in the hazy heat of afternoon, but the half-breed doubted that it was what it seemed. And after a brief exchange of glances with the crouching Poco Oso, he knew that the Apache also sensed that the front of the ravaged law office was under surveillance.

"We ain't locked up anymore, but we're still prisoners, uh?" Larsen asked.

"We know of one feller who was in no condition to ride," Edge muttered.

"And that Earl Smithson will be itchin' to make you and the Indian pay."

"We have to figure he ain't on his toes," the half-breed growled, interrupting his concentration on the broad, deserted street and the blank façade of the buildings on the far side to direct his slit-eyed gaze first at Poco Oso and then at Larsen, who was still gripping the rope that bound von Scheel's wrists. "The saloon is where we have to get to. I'll go first, to the right. You go to the left soon as I'm clear of the doorway. You get over here fast and give us covering fire if there's any shooting."

"Damnit, there could be a dozen sharpshooters in positions to start blastin' at this place in the event any of us shows ourselves," Larsen pointed out sourly.

"You got anything in mind except worry about what could be, feller?"

The marshal scowled.

"I'm ready, white eyes," the Apache said.

Edge dropped into a crouch as the brave moved from the window to the opposite side of the doorway. Both shot a glance at Larsen, who sustained his scowl but nodded as he let go of von Scheel. The German backed into a corner, where he would be safe from any stray bullets that found entrance through doorway or window. With his hands bound at his back, he had to try to blink the sweat beads from his eyes.

"Move!"

The half-breed powered himself forward, snatching up his Frontier Colt and lunging out into the brilliant sunlight. He headed for the dry-goods store to the right of the saloon. The Apache was a half-second behind him, grabbing his ancient Navy Colt and making a dash for the Chinese laundry across the alley to the left of the Mother Lode. A moment later the lawman showed himself briefly in the doorway to claim his fancy-handled Remington, then ducked back to stand in the place Edge had vacated.

The half-breed was tensely aware of the risk that he and the others were running. But he calculated it to be a lot less dangerous than Larsen's anxious estimate because those citizens of Thunderhead who carried grudges against the Apaches would be riding for Santa Luiz. And among those who remained in town, how many cared one way or the other about the four men who had escaped from their cells? At the same time how many of those who felt Hoy and his followers were doing the right thing were prepared to kill, and risk being killed, in a gunfight with the escapees? He guessed that few would be ready to take a hand in a dangerous situation that was basically none of their concern.

He and the Apache were a quarter of the way across the street toward their objective when a man shrieked: "Shit, they're loose!"

It was Earl Smithson, his voice barely revealing the fact that his position was behind a window of the saloon before the glass shattered across the street in a sun-glinting spray as he blasted a bullet through it. The shot from rifle was a mere reflex, the wild explosion of a surprised man.

Edge had no idea where it went, felt no rush of air or thud of impact as he veered from his straight course to begin zigzagging toward his objective. Out of the corner of his eye, he saw the Apache adopt the same tactic. The man with the bullet-holed feet had a repeater: against the thud of footfalls on the dusty street Edge heard the series of metallic clicks as a spent shell was ejected and a fresh round jacked into the breech.

He and Poco Oso were now three-quarters of the way across the street. Both fired their revolvers at the shattered window, but the range was too far for a handgun, and as they were running in crouches, the chances for accuracy were further reduced. Thus the bullets merely smacked into the façade of the saloon, chips of which exploded at the points of impact. But the spurts of muzzle smoke from the two Colts and the reports of the shells leaving the muzzles did cause Earl Smithson to take the time to duck into cover.

A moment later, however, the rifle sent another shot through the window . . . and Poco Oso went hard to the ground.

"Larsen, you bastard!" the half-breed said. But the words were rasped through clenched teeth and were heard by their speaker's ears alone.

Then he saw that the Apache was getting to his feet and skidded to a halt, turning to face the shattered window, half-crouched and with his feet splayed. He thrust the Frontier Colt forward in his right hand, index finger to the trigger, and began to fan the hammer. He was less than twenty feet from the front of the saloon, and amid the fast series of reports from bullets blasted in through the smashed window, he heard the sounds of the repeater action again. He also heard the less frenetic cracks of a handgun being fired.

Then the Apache was up on his feet again and running, veering away from the front of the laundry to make for the batwings behind the hitching rail.

The Frontier Colt rattled, empty.

Meanwhile, Larsen continued to fire methodically from the doorway of the law office, his shots pocking the areas below, above, and to the sides of the window.

Through the dust raised by running feet and drifting gun smoke, Edge saw the face of Earl Smithson. Deeply inscribed with pain and hatred, anger and triumph, he rested his cheek against the stock of a Winchester rifle and took careful aim at the half-breed who held an empty gun in his hand.

"Apache's gone and now it's your turn, Apache lover!"

But Poco Oso had either been faking a gunshot wound or had taken the dive to avoid one. For he showed no sign of being hurt, as he ducked under the rail and lunged into another dive to smash open the batwings with his shoulder and crash into the saloon on his belly.

"Sonofafrigginbitch!" Smithson shrieked, swinging the Winchester away from Edge to try to draw a bead on the Apache, who was sliding across the sawdust-strewn floor. He squeezed the trigger.

The hammer of Larsen's Remington clicked forward at the instant, but the firing pin hit only an empty shell case. Edge powered himself forward, thrusting the Colt into the holster. He raised his leading leg to put his booted foot on the ledge of the smashed window and launched himself into a flying tackle.

Smithson was seated on a chair to one side of the window and four feet back from it. He was twisted from the waist up, his face showing only terror now as he stared at Poco Oso and fumbled an attempt to pump the Winchester's action again. His panicked shot at a man he thought was dead had missed its target. And the Apache had completed his slide and was knocking aside chairs, as he struggled to get his feet. The old Colt was back in his weapons belt and he had drawn the knife.

But the blade of Edge's razor was the first to find the yielding flesh of the man trapped by his injuries in the chair.

The half-breed drew the razor from the neck pouch while he was in mid-air. He made a sideway, slashing move with it a moment before Smithson was aware of the danger from a source other than the Indian. Thus, it was no more than an instant before he died that the big miner saw the instrument of his death when he snapped his head around. He saw the blade of the razor extended from the fist of the man diving at him, then felt its bite into the flesh of his throat. He began a scream of horror, but its sound was drowned in the blood from his severed jugular vein. Perhaps he felt the warmth of running blood on his skin, or perhaps there

114

was not even time for this sensation—because before he and his chair tipped backward under the impact of Edge's shoulder on his chest, his neck was gashed from ear to ear. In the final seconds of his life he was in the grip of the terror of dying, a terror that swamped all other feeling.

He was a corpse before he thudded to the floor and rolled out of the overturned chair. His wide eyes glazed and showed no reaction as the weight of his killer fell onto him.

Silence again enveloped the town of Thunderhead, but it lasted for no more than a couple of seconds, as Larsen yelled from across the street: "You men all right?"

"You hear us complaining?" Edge shouted, as he got to his feet and saw the anger that contorted the face and stiffened the body of Poco Oso. Lowering his voice, he murmured: "Though it appears this feller ain't the only one cut up over what happened."

"I did not need your help, white eyes," the Apache hissed, looking from the blade of his knife to the dead Earl Smithson and then to the half-breed. "A man with so much hate for the Apaches, he deserved to die by hand of Apache."

"Keep on being mad at me, feller," Edge said evenly.

The handsome brave maintained his rage at a high level for what seemed like a long time. Then the tension drained out of him, and he put the knife back in its sheath. He began to hand-brush the sawdust off his buckskin clothes. "You want we no longer be friends, white eyes? That okay with me. After you give word to the Apache killer."

Edge stooped to wipe off the blood of the razor on the pants of the dead man, then slid it back in the neck pouch and nodded. "That's fine," he said. "After what this feller called me."

"Call you?" the brave sneered.

"Apache lover. I ain't never had any *fruitful* friendships."

"I do not understand you," Poco Oso said, disinterested, as Larsen pushed von Scheel through the batwings.

"And I ain't going to help you, feller," the half-breed answered, as he reloaded his Colt. "I don't bend over backwards—or forwards—for any man."

Chapter Nine

"You men in the saloon!"

Edge, Poco Oso, and Larsen all whirled with guns tracking ahead of their eyes. Through the broken window they saw that a number of men were now out on the street, gathering into a group at its center, directly in front of the Mother Lode. The half-breed recognized four of them as the men who had been playing cards in the saloon before the prospect of trouble sent them scuttling outside.

Like the majority of the score or so of men who had converged onto the street from all directions, they were still nervous. But there was the strength of resolution in the way all the men took up their stances and peered at the bullet-ridden façade of the saloon. From the ages of thirty to sixty, most of them had the soft hands, fresh complexions, and relatively clean clothing of men who did not have to do heavy manual labor to earn a living: storekeepers, clerks, and businessmen. Here and there appeared a tougher-looking, less tidily attired man: a leather-aproned blacksmith, a stocky man with paint on his hands and pants and bare torso, and the biggest and broadest of all, the town butcher, with animal blood staining his coveralls.

If any of them were armed with guns, the weapons were hidden. But the butcher, who was spokesman for the group, carried a meat cleaver at his side. Larsen began hurriedly to reload his Remington while the Apache instinctively drew his knife.

"Earl Smithson was party to an attempt to divert due process of law!" the marshal yelled over the tops of the batwings.

"We don't give a shit about Smithson!" the butcher countered.

"Remember the ladies, Mr. Bayless," lisped a meek-looking little man.

Bayless nodded and directed a contrite glance up and down the street before returning his glaring attention to the men in the saloon. "What him and the rest of the men off the claims get up to is their own concern. Us townfolk just supply their needs."

There were nods and grunts of agreement, and Bayless expressed mild satisfaction, obviously pleased with his appointment as spokesman and the way he was handling the chore.

"Feller," Edge drawled, moving closer to the window. "You got something to say, just say it. We don't have the time to listen to speeches."

Bayless glowered.

118

One of the former card players urged: "Yeah, George. Get it said."

"All right, gunslinger! Want you to know you ain't welcome here in Thunderhead. The same goes for the Apache. And you, Marshal. We already had a bellyful of trouble on account of Indians and men that figure Indians gotta be treated like they was whites. So we just wanna say get outta our town and don't come back."

"No sweat," Edge responded.

"It's only you men that are holdin' us up from leavin'." Larsen augmented the half-breed's meaning.

"That's just fine and dandy. But just don't try to take anythin' that don't belong to you. On account of we have to make a livin' outta Ray Hoy and the rest of the men that rode for Santa Luiz."

This said, the group broke up.

"What does he mean?" Poco Oso asked.

"Figure they took the marshal's horse as well as our mounts, feller," Edge answered, while he watched the crowd disperse. "Maybe even the drummer's team. Only overlooked our hand-guns. It's a long walk to the mission." He spat on the sawdust floor. "And we could get there with sore feet and short of arms."

"Hey, the gunsmith's got my Winchester!" Larsen remembered. He made a motion to push out through the batwings but pulled up short.

"It's on the seat of the foreigner's wagon, Marshal," a man passing the saloon doorway supplied. "Fitted the new trigger spring and unbent the hammer like you wanted. And right now Charlie Hill is hitchin' the team to the

119

wagon out back of his livery. Luck to you white men. Apaches ain't to our likin', and we got nothin' against them old folks over at Santa Luiz."

"But you ain't prepared to lift a finger to help them," Larsen growled with sour scorn.

"It ain't our trouble," the Thunderhead gunsmith answered dully. "And them old folks only ever sell to us. Never do buy."

"People like you make me friggin' sick!" the lawman snarled.

"So let's head for the mission," the half-breed said, as he swung a leg over the ledge of the smashed window. "Lots of other sick people there, one way or another."

After the gunsmith had turned into his store, the single curved street was once again deserted. But as the four unwelcome visitors to town made their way to the livery stable, the half-breed, the lawman, and the Indian were aware of being watched. The German was insensitive to everything except his own depression. The piano player in the dance hall once again began to float the melancholy music out into the hot afternoon air, as if in sympathy with von Scheel's misery.

At the rear of Charlie's Livery Stable, all was as the gunsmith had promised. The fed and rested two-horse team was in the traces of the cloyingly smelling town wagon. The repaired, cleaned, and oiled Winchester was on the seat.

"You and the Apache take the seat," Larsen said, after claiming his rifle. "Me and my prisoner will ride in the back."

And this was how they rode, as Edge took the

reins to drive the wagon along the alley beside the stable and turned to head down the slope of the empty street, then out onto the open trail that intersected five miles away with the trail toward Santa Luiz.

"I think the white eyes with badge does not trust me," the brave said softly, as the wagon rolled past the town marker at an easy pace, the hooves of the two horses and the turning wheels raising dust. "He is afraid, maybe, that I will take it upon myself to deal with Apache killer."

"I can hear what you're sayin'," Larsen growled, "and what you're sayin' has crossed my mind, Indian. But I figure you'd like best of all to waste me and Edge some way and be a regular hero to your people by takin' them my prisoner, alive and kickin'."

Von Scheel groaned his reaction to this terrifying prospect. The marshal, who had become increasingly short-tempered since his easy capture of the killer had turned sour, snarled at the German to shut up. Edge, who had been deep in thought as he drove the wagon out of town, sensed the Apache watching him, and he responded to the faintly quizzical gaze of the black eyes with an ice-cold glance.

"Figure you could have handled the feller in the saloon back there," he said evenly, as he resumed his apparently casual survey of the surrounding terrain. "So I still owe you for the snake. But what I said then still goes. You aim a gun at me again, kill me or you're dead. Same with the knife."

"I need only to be told something once, white eyes. I do not forget."

"Just like elephants, feller. And they get to live to a great age."

Most of the time Edge forgot only what he chose to forget, but occasionally what was left of his conscience pushed to the forefront of his mind certain memories of the distant past that were invariably charged with pain and anguish. Like the incident in his childhood that had led to an aversion to having a gun aimed at him—an aversion which went beyond the natural fear of such a situation. He and Jamie had been fooling with a rifle that should not have been loaded, and the bullet that exploded from the muzzle shattered the younger brother's leg and left him a cripple for the rest of his tragically short life.

But as he rode the wagon now, with three other men who for a while were wrapped up in their own thoughts, the mind of the impassive half-breed began to taunt him with many other memories, triggered by the dull-sounding words of the gunsmith back in Thunderhead: *It ain't our trouble*.

The man had spoken the truth, and in detaching themselves from the potential death and destruction at Santa Luiz, he and the other men were acting according to the basic tenet by which Edge lived his own life. He had based his loner's philosophy on hard-learned lessons, which had been violently implanted in his memory.

So why was he going back to Santa Luiz?

Chief Ahone had charged him with finding and bringing back Fritz von Scheel—albeit showing the Apache's inbred distrust of whites by having Poco Oso trail him and watch that he did as ordered. And now the wanted man was on his way to his appointment with fate, escorted by Marshal Larsen, who considered it his sworn duty to do everything possible to protect both his prisoner and the old-timers at the former mission, and accompanied by the son of Ahone, who as an Apache brave had perhaps a more powerful reason to see that the doomed mass killer kept the appointment. In such potentially volatile circumstances, made even more so by the presence of the Apache-haters from Thunderhead, the reactions of the chief and their effect upon the diseased and crippled old-timers of Santa Luiz were hardly likely to be influenced one way or the other by the presence or absence of Edge.

So why the hell was he electing to ignore the lessons of the harsh past—to head directly toward another rendezvous with violence? Why go where it was certain that he would have to put his life on the line by taking part in trouble that was not of his making?

"You know what that Bayless character meant, Edge?" Larsen asked suddenly from the strong-smelling rear of the wagon.

"About what?"

"Thunderhead folks havin' had a bellyful of Indian trouble."

"I'm a stranger around here," the half-breed answered, as he took the makings of a cigarette from a shirt pocket. He knew, as he had known from the start, exactly why he was along for this ride: because he had promised the German drummer to kill him rather than allow the Apaches to take him alive; because, also, he

123

owed the massively built Ray Hoy for locking him in a cell; and because of the opportunity at Santa Luiz for more wanton killing—the kind that had occurred when he had robbed Poco Oso of the opportunity to be first to put a blade in the flesh of Earl Smithson . . . ?

The Indian began to speak and thus gave Edge a chance to curb his morbid reflection on this aspect of his choice.

"It happened a short while ago," the brave said. "There were two men with badges in the town of Thunderhead then. Good and fair men. It was not so bad for the Apache. Many worked there. Doing such things as they have done at the Mission of Santa Luiz. But then one of the women of low morals from the dance hall was killed. She was found in one of the old tunnels in the hills. Naked and staked to the earth. Her tongue was cut out, her breasts were cut off, and that part of a woman that gives a man most pleasure—it was filled with the ashes of burned wood."

Edge struck a match on the butt of his holstered Colt and lit his cigarette.

"You Apaches sure know how to make a person suffer," Larsen growled, and von Scheel made a retching sound.

"It *was* Apaches who did this thing," Poco Oso allowed without emotion. "Two Mimbrenos, outcasts from their tribe. But they were provoked to hatred of the woman. For she made them drunk with liquor, aroused their lust with her nakedness, then laughed when she denied them."

"No white men would have done what they

did to get back at her," Larsen put in defensively.

"You asked question and I am giving you answer," the Apache countered. "I am not speaking on behalf of these braves."

"You're an Apache!"

"And you're a lousy listener, feller," Edge put in.

The lawman grunted a sour response.

The Indian continued: "The men with badges locked the Mimbrenos in place where we were prisoners. To protect them from white eyes who are also drunk and want to beat them for lusting after woman who is not a squaw. Then braves are set free and told to leave. But they do not. Instead, lay in wait for woman who caused trouble. And do to her what I have told.

"They are captured by braves of my father's Tonto tribe, who believe Chief Ahone is right to try to live in peace with the white eyes. Who give them back to men with badges in the town of Thunderhead. On vow that the Mimbrenos will have justice same as if they are not Apaches.

"But men who rob the earth of gold in the hills do not agree with promise made by men with badges. There is shooting and burning at the place where prisoners are held. And men with badges lay down their arms. They do not lack courage. They do this because they have no wish to kill their white eyes brothers. To protect Apaches they know are murderers and will die soon. So men with badges get on their horses and ride away, never to return. But they would need to travel many miles until they could no longer hear the screams of the Mimbrenos."

"Got a taste of their own medicine, uh?" Larsen asked rhetorically, but there was a strained quality about his apparent satisfaction with the fate of the Apache murderers.

When Edge glanced at Poco Oso, he saw that the Indian had also detected this false note.

"First they sliced off their manhoods. A little at a time. Then forced them to watch as the pieces of flesh were tossed to hungry dogs. Next their toes and fingers were removed. Their ears and their noses. They were staked out in the manner of the woman they killed and the men relieved themselves onto their faces. Lastly, fires were lit on their bellies.

"They suffered their agonies from the setting of one sun until the rising of the next."

There was a long pause after the brave had finished his story. Then Larsen said: "Some whites have learned some real mean tricks from you Apaches."

"There was not whiskey and women of low morals to tempt the weakest of Apache braves before the white eyes came," Poco Oso responded.

"Yeah, all you redskins were angels without any damn wings, I don't bet. Appears to me those Mimbrenos got poetic justice, wouldn't you say so, Edge?"

"Some Thunderhead people sure seem to be well versed in how to hand it out," the halfbreed answered sardonically. He steered the wagon around a curve in the trail and saw the end of the spur ahead.

"Dammit!" Larsen snarled. "It ain't no kiddin' matter. And I'm not speakin' what's in my mind. Them Thunderhead lawmen were a damn disgrace to the badges they wore. They should've made a stand and died if necessary. Don't matter what their prisoners were."

Edge's estimation of the marshal from Santa Fe, which had been high at first meeting and had then gone into a decline, rose again. He hauled on the reins to halt the team, dropped his cigarette to the trail, and jumped down, crushing out its fire beneath a boot heel.

"Hey, why the stop?" Larsen wanted to know, while the Apache eyed the half-breed quizzically.

"We're just a mile away from where we're headed," Edge answered. "Much closer, and even if the wagon ain't seen or heard, it'll likely be smelled."

Larsen pushed open the rear doors and emerged. He paused to give the bound von Scheel a hand to get out of the wagon, then scowled and brushed at his clothing as he complained: "Damnit, I stink to high heaven from just ridin' in back with the stuff."

Poco Oso climbed down from the seat and said coldly: "It will save expense of flowers for your grave, white eyes. Should you try to trick Chief Ahone."

"There vill be no trick, Apache," the German said miserably, as the lawman frowned with anger at the Indian. But there was contempt in his puffy green eyes as they switched their attention from Edge to Larsen and back again. "If

127

this had been vhat vas intended, you vould still be in the prison cell. Or dead."

Larsen whirled as if to snarl an angry denial at von Scheel. But the move was really a feint, giving him the opportunity to pump the action of the Winchester as he gripped it with both hands, the German being only the apparent target of his temper. A second later his actual intention was clear as, in a hunched, sideways-on stance, he aimed the rifle from the hip at the Apache—along half the length of the wagon. "I'll kill you if I have to, Indian!" the lawman rasped.

The brave was taken by surprise. But he recovered quickly and turned his head slowly to look away from Larsen and direct another of his quizzical gazes at the half-breed, asking, "You knew of this?"

"No, feller."

"You do something about it?"

"Damnit, get his gun and knife, mister!" Larsen ordered. "If you don't, I'll kill him for sure. Ain't we got enough hostiles to deal with at Santa Luiz without takin' in another one who's likely to jump us any second?"

Edge was standing close to the brave. Now he moved closer, but behind him, to reach for his weapons belt and take from it the old Colt and the knife.

Larsen grunted with satisfaction and von Scheel sighed with relief. Poco Oso hissed a single Apache word in the tone of a curse.

Edge tossed the weapons far out into a patch of brush and said to the brave: "If it hadn't been him, it'd been me."

"I thought you had trust in me, white eyes."

The half-breed shook his head. "Make it a point never to trust anybody."

"Let's go," Larsen growled, gesturing with the rifle, which was still leveled toward the Indian. "Before it's too late to help the folks at Santa Luiz."

As Poco Oso turned around to begin walking away from the wagon in the direction of the former mission, he said: "If the white eyes from the town have been seen by my father's sentries, it is already too late. Chief Ahone will think I have failed and the man Edge commanded the attack."

Larsen signaled with a nod of his head for von Scheel to walk in front of him. But the German was careful not to get between the muzzle of the rifle and the broad back of the Indian. Edge fell in beside the lawman and lit a freshly rolled cigarette.

"I'll give you another 'if,' Indian," the tall, thin, black-clad marshal countered. "If there'd been a fight between that many whites and that many Apaches, we'd have heard the gunfire. Ain't that so, Edge?"

"Figure those Thunderhead fellers realized they left town in too much of a hurry," the half-breed answered. "Be kicking their heels now. Waiting for nightfall before making their move."

"Damn right," Larsen agreed, as the quartet of men entered the late afternoon shade of the ravine a few yards beyond the two-armed signpost.

"Night is another world from day," Poco Oso

said levelly, his brand of confidence in a much lower key than that of the lawman. "My people are at home in both. Few white eyes are so."

Larsen laughed harshly. "Quit tryin' to scare us, Indian. Or I might get nervous enough to blast you into another world."

The brave glanced scornfully over his shoulder, and Larsen's mirth faded. He glared his anger at Poco Oso. Then he snapped his head around to face Edge, as the half-breed reached out a hand and placed it under the barrel of the rifle—to tilt it skyward.

"One shot is likely to fire off a whole lot more, feller. If it's like we figure. And the Apaches still have mission control."

Chapter Ten

They were a little over halfway into the two-hundred-yard-long ravine when the Apache scowled his dissatisfaction that Larsen had taken the half-breed's point. For now the chance was gone to goad the lawman into exploding a gunshot that would warn Ahone and his braves of men approaching Santa Luiz from the east.

Edge read this in the expression of Poco Oso just before the Apache swung his head to face forward again, perhaps contemplating a sudden and suicidal attempt to turn the tables on the white men in the hope that Larsen would blast at him instinctively. Then he would die content in the knowledge that the sacrifice was of use to his people. The half-breed abruptly lengthened his stride to come up close behind the German.

"What's the idea?" Larsen asked, but before

the demand was fully uttered, it was already partially answered. For Edge had drawn the Colt from his holster and pressed it into the nape of von Scheel's neck.

A strangled cry squeezed from the German's constricted throat as he came to a sudden halt. The Apache and the lawman also pulled up short, equally shocked and confused by the half-breed's action.

Edge nodded toward the end of the ravine, where the sloping trail seemed to be cut off by the reddening sky of evening between the rock faces. "If Ahone ain't got sentries up on the rims who've seen us already, there'll be Apaches positioned to spot us soon as we crest that rise."

"Don't tell anyone what you're gonna do before you do it, will you?" Larsen growled.

"Vhy you hold gun on me?" von Scheel whined. "You made me promise."

Poco Oso nodded his understanding of another part of the half-breed's plan while the marshal continued to scowl in confusion. "He is man of his word . . . to white eyes," the brave averred. "My people want you to suffer much, Apache killer. So it is not me but you, threatened with quick death, who will gain our captors safe passage across the ground held by my people."

"Hey, that's smart," Larsen allowed.

Von Sheel had to swallow hard to shift the constricting fear from his throat and ask: "But vhat vill ve do vehn ve are at Santa Luiz? Have you thought about that, Herr Edge?"

"That ain't my problem, feller. My job is just

132

to bring you there. You want to start moving again?"

He applied a little pressure to the gun against the sweating neck, and the German did as requested.

"You as well, Indian," Larsen growled, and again leveled his Winchester at the back of Poco Oso. "Double insurance," he added.

And this was how they emerged onto the highest point of the trail at the end of the ravine—two abreast, with the guns of the pair behind threatening instant death to the pair in front.

The sun was starting to set now, its leading arc already below the ridges to the southwest, its crimson light casting long shadows across the large basin in which the adobe buildings of Santa Luiz were clustered. None of the shadows were cast by human forms, either on the encircling slopes or down in the oasislike settlement. But to the four men who emerged from the ravine and started out on the trail's downgrade, the almost palpable silence in the cooling air of the mountain evening had an eerie quality that seemed to transmit a tacit message of lurking danger.

With the heat of the day almost gone, feelings of tension started to squeeze beads of moisture from their every pore, pasting their clothing to their flesh and annoyingly trickling across their brows and over their cheeks. Their eyes flicked back and forth, raking over every pocket of cover on the slopes and along the jagged line of every sandstone ridge, searching the blank walls and unmoving vegetation of Santa Luiz, seeking a puff of dust, a glint of sunlight on gunmetal, or a hurried snatching back of a hand, foot, or head. But neither Apaches nor whites revealed their presence as the four men drew closer to the community, walking at a funereal pace dictated by the two prisoners.

"Where the hell is everybody?" Larsen whispered tensely.

"When my people are ready to be seen, you will see them," Poco Oso answered. He was gripped by the same degree of anxiety as the lawman. It was seen in his rigid gait and was heard in the thickness of his voice.

"Perhaps there is nobody left alive," von Scheel suggested huskily. "Perhaps the men from Thunderhead vere seen. And the old people vere slaughtered. The Apache Indians are gone."

"I'll put my money on your feller telling it the way it is," Edge said evenly.

"So why ain't any of the old folks showin' themselves?" Larsen wanted to know.

"Maybe they're even more spooked than you are," the half-breed offered with an icy grin that parted his lips a fraction but did not touch the glinting slits of his eyes. "Scared stiff."

"Stiff from being dead, I think," von Scheel disagreed. "And the Apache Indians are hiding in Santa Luiz. Waiting until ve valk into their trap."

"For four fellers who could have no future, we're spending a lot of time trying to look into it."

"What else you wanna do, Edge? Play a spellin' bee or somethin'?"

134

"All I want is to get this job done."

"And you think my people will allow you to leave after you have cheated them, white eyes?" Again the Apache had contempt in his tone as the quartet reached the foot of the slope and started along the level stretch of trail toward Santa Luiz. "If they are denied the right to punish the Apache killer, you will be made to suffer in his place."

"Just said my piece about trying to look into the future."

They were close enough to the buildings and the greenery now to hear the almost musical sound of the running spring water in the old mission church. But then the surrounding stillness was shattered by less pleasant sounds: the sharp crack of a rifle shot and the crash of metal on rock as the bullet ricocheted, followed by three progressively fainter echoes, as the shot and its effect resounded among the ridges where it had been fired from.

Von Scheel gasped his terror, and all four men came to a halt a few yards short of the aspen grove at the center of the plaza. The German was held rigid from head to toe by the fear of death. But Edge, Larsen, and Poco Oso turned and looked up at the jagged southwestern ridge, where three mounted Apaches were silhouetted on the skyline against the trailing arc of the sun.

Chief Ahone's distinctive sartorial style of city suit and Stetson hat marked him plainly as the central member of the trio. But it was the brave to the right who cupped his hands to his mouth to yell a question in the Apache tongue,

135

the words resounding among the peaks in the same manner as the rifle shot.

"Tell him to speak American, or this feller gets it in the neck. Here and now." While Edge snarled out the order amid the still-echoing voice of the brave, he pressed the muzzle of the Colt more firmly against the flesh of the wretched von Scheel, forcing the man's head forward.

"You tell him, white eyes!" Poco Oso snarled softly.

"Bye-bye, feller," Edge murmured. "This way has to beat torture and hanging both."

"I tell him!" the son of Chief Ahone blurted. "And answer him."

"*Mein Gott,* I am dying a thousand times," the German gasped.

"I know how you feel," Larsen muttered, as he and Edge, quickly glanced around. More Apaches, in groups of three, heeled their ponies forward from behind the ridges. Eleven such trios were now equidistantly spaced around the rim of the basin.

"It is ordered you speak in the tongue of the white eyes!" Poco Oso was shouting through the horn of his cupped hands, as the braves showed themselves but halted their ponies only feet away from the cover that had previously concealed them. "Or Apache killer will die quickly from bullet! This is answer to what you ask!"

All the braves had drawn their rifles, stocks resting on their thighs and barrels aiming skyward. But as soon as Edge's threat was related to them, many of the Indians threw their weapons to their shoulders.

"Damnit to hell!" Larsen growled.

"Hold it!" Edge snapped, his words in unison with an order shrieked in Apache by Ahone's spokesman.

The rifles were ported again, and the tense silence returned to the basin, while the chief could be seen leaning to the side of his pony, talking to the brave on his right. This brave put his hands to his mouth again. "Your father, Chief Ahone, asks what is meaning of what he sees, Poco Oso?"

"Tell him we want in to the mission," Edge responded to the captive Indian's bleakly expectant gaze. "After that, a truce talk."

The message was conveyed, followed by a longer pause than before. The city-suited Apache chief sat astride his pony in a contemplative attitude, then spoke curtly to the brave on his right, who translated: "Your father, Chief Ahone, agrees to this, Poco Oso! He warns we will take lives of all if Apache killer dies quickly!"

There was no shouted order on this occasion. When Ahone and his flanking braves withdrew into cover behind the ridges, the rest of the encircling Apaches did likewise.

"Holy cow!" Larsen exclaimed after expelling his pent-up breath through his teeth. "I made it thirty-three Indians up in them hills."

"Check, feller," Edge agreed, applying gentle pressure to the back of von Scheel's neck, which was enough to set him moving toward the cover

137

of the former mission church. "Which means he didn't send back to the Rancheria for reinforcements."

Poco Oso snorted his scorn, as he too started for the closed doorway under the bell tower on the far side of the plaza. "There are more than enough, white eyes. And I have not overlooked the haters of Apache nation who come from Thunderhead. Your truce talk will serve no purpose. You will all be killed. And this because of one man who will die anyway. By hand of my people or your own."

The door of the mission church was eased open a few inches, then all the way. The six-member council of old-timers who represented the citizens of Santa Luiz peered despairingly through the fast-gathering dusk at the group of four, who halted on the other side of the threshold.

"Welcome back to you, Mr. Edge," the tall, thin, one-eyed Phil Frazier greeted dully. "You done like you promised, and you don't deserve to die for that. But I reckon this Apache is right. We're all gonna die." His good eye glared at von Scheel and Poco Oso. Then he nodded to Larsen.

The lame Lloyd DeHart asked: "What was that he said about folks from Thunderhead?"

"He said not to count on them, feller," Edge growled. "And maybe he's right."

"How's that?" Larsen asked, fast and anxious.

"Why should they help people who ain't hospitable?"

The line of old-timers were all perplexed.

"Invite them folks in, you dunderheads!"

Amelia Randall chided from within the mission church.

"Obliged, ma'am," the half-breed answered, as the line of old-timers fell back, and he urged von Scheel with the Colt to go through the doorway. "Outside in the mountains on a night like this, a man could catch his death."

Chapter Eleven

It had gotten to be full night now. The newcomers entered the church, and as the door was closed at their backs, candles were lit.

In the flickering light it could be seen how the building had been transformed from its former religious purpose to meet the needs of the sick and the old, who chose to place their faith in the healing powers of God's water rather than the guiding light of His spirit. All the pews had been removed from their original positions and many of them remodeled into high-sided beds, which were aligned along the south wall in the manner of a hospital ward. Others had been totally dismantled to provide lumber for the partitions that subdivided a section of the north wall into cubicles separated with fabric curtains. Here and there a curtain was not closed, and metal bathtubs could be seen.

There were four stoves down what had once

been the central aisle. But tonight only one was burning, and the big two-handled cauldrons and some less bulky water carriers were stacked neatly at the foot of the bell tower just beyond the doorway.

The spring that was the reason for the resurgence of Santa Luiz after its failure as a mission was at the base of the west wall, in the area where the altar and pulpit would have been. The crystal-clear water emerged from the ground and trickled down a smooth stone into a small pool. The four tense travel-weary men gratefully drank cups of the sweet-tasting, refreshingly cool water, while the fifty or so old-timers silently watched and waited for some sign or word that might mean their ordeal was close to being over.

"Damn," Larsen muttered after he had drunk his fill. "Someone oughta be watchin' in case the Apaches try anythin'."

"Jonas Cole and Ed Dalby are up at the top of the bell tower," Frazier said. "It was them told us you men were headin' down the trail. We figured you knew what you was doin', so we all stayed real quiet."

"Didn't wanna do nothin' to stir up them Injuns we knew was in the hills," the gaunt bearded John Newman added. "You boys sure did take a chance walkin' down here like that, large as life."

"We was all prayin' for you," a woman called weakly from one of the beds. She was the only regular bedridden patient of the makeshift hospital section of the mission. Everybody else was on their feet or seated on bedding, which had been brought from the houses and spread on the floor.

"Took a vote," Frazier explained, as Amelia Randall gathered up the cups and withdrew from the poolside where the Santa Luiz councilmen and the quartet of outsiders were grouped. "Everyone was of the opinion we'd feel better about the way things are if we was all here together in this place."

The bald and stocky Jake Donabie said quickly: "But we're ready to go where you want and do whatever you say to help, Mr. Edge."

Spoken words of agreement and several nods rippled among the large group of anxious old-timers behind the councilmen. And the gray-haired Amelia Randall expanded on their feeling: "We're real grateful you done what the Indians asked and come back with the unfortunate Mr. Von."

The German obviously appreciated the woman's sympathetic attitude and seemed about to correct her impression of his name. But Marshal Larsen got in ahead of him, and explained sourly: "You people oughta be thankful to him for that. But don't look to him for any more good work—unless it's to help himself."

This drew exclamations of anxious surprise from the audience, to which the half-breed showed no response, as he finished rolling a cigarette and lit it.

Larsen sighed and reclaimed the attention of the worried old people. "This situation is my problem now. As a marshal of the Territory of New Mexico and because this here man"—he gestured with his Winchester toward von Scheel—"was under arrest for murder by me when Edge and the Indian come to Thunderhead and told me about the way things was here."

"Murder?" Arnie Prescott exclaimed, leaning hard on the stick that eased the burden of his clubfoot. This clearly spoken query silenced the mutterings of the crowd.

While Larsen told of the killings at Los Alamos, Edge smoked the cigarette and rubbed the back of a hand across the bristles on his jaw, as he watched the handsome Apache brave struggle to check his mounting impatience.

"Old and blind?"

"How awful!"

"That's terrible!"

"He ain't nothin' but a monster!"

"Mr. Von, how could you . . . ?"

The responses to the lawman's story of the Los Alamos murders came fast and furious, then were abruptly curtailed when Lloyd DeHart snarled: "So why powwow with the 'Paches? Iffen this guy is due to be hung up Santa Fe way, just turn him over to Ahone's bunch and our trouble's over."

It was impossible to tell what proportion of old-timers were for DeHart's solution and how many were against, during the short, heated, confused discussion it triggered.

"This is how it must be, white eyes!" Poco Oso shouted above the noise of arguing voices. "To hold fast to the laws of your people because of this evil man will mean that you all will die!"

144

"Shut up!" Larsen snarled, whirling to aim his rifle at the determined Apache.

Edge turned too, drew the Colt and smashed it against the temple and forehead of the brave.

Poco Oso groaned in the sudden silence, dropped hard to his knees, and pitched forward.

Larsen transferred his frowning gaze from the unconscious Indian to the heavily bristled face of the half-breed and rasped: "You sure are full of damn surprises, mister!"

"That's one Injun done for," the morose Elmer Randall muttered. "But there's a whole lot more out in the hills waitin' to hear about Von here."

"My name is von *Scheel*," the German said dully. "In the language of—"

"Keep your mouth shut, killer!" DeHart snarled. "You think we care you got some high-hatted double-barrel name?"

"Why, mister?" the lawman asked, his anger abating. "You said your job was finished. So it's down to me now. And I was countin' on usin' him to do a deal."

"You reckon them people from Thunderhead didn't like what they saw here and took off back to town?" Jake Donabie put in.

Some of the old-timers were as eager as he to have this answered. But many more shared Larsen's expectancy as they gazed at Edge.

The half-breed ground out the glowing ashes of his cigarette under a boot heel. "The men from town are out there. They're too eager to have an excuse to kill Apaches, so they're not going to turn tail and run home while the

145

chance of some slaughter is still high. . . . Laid out this Apache because he saved my life this morning and I owed him."

"Mister, I'm glad you ain't indebted to me," a wizened man with a deformed right arm muttered.

"He was itching to help his people get their hands on this feller. Scratching that itch could've got him killed."

"You have not forgotten your promise to me?" von Scheel asked miserably, obviously with little hope of ever leaving Santa Luiz alive.

"Hey, the Injuns are comin' over the ridges again!" one of the watchers at the top of the bell tower called. There was an eerie quality in his voice as it traveled downward and then spread across the cavernous interior of the former church.

Old women clung to their elderly husbands, and strained words of reassurance were given in response to terrified exclamations.

"If your invite to truce talks was to gain time, mister, we ain't used it wisely," Larsen growled.

"Ahone never would have done any deal to keep his son alive unless he got von Scheel into the bargain. You have any other ideas?"

Larsen grimaced. "All the way from Thunderhead and ever since we been here, I was countin' on Ray Hoy and them others that figure the only good Indians are dead ones."

Edge clicked his tongue against the roof of his mouth and nodded. "That's the right idea, feller," he said, as he turned and began to walk down the aisle, passing the stoves. "And after all that shouting when we first got here, we have to figure they're counting on us."

He pulled open the door and stepped out into the cool, brightly moonlit night. His narrowed eyes raked over those sections of the encircling ridges that were not obstructed by buildings and trees. The Apaches he could see were mounted on ponies in the familiar groups of three, the rifles ported to their thighs.

He had been seen emerging from the doorway and a bird call was used to signal this to the more distant braves. He moved across the front of the building and turned. The moon caused the neat crosses marking the graves of those old people who had not been cured by the clear air and the cool spring water to cast shadows.

Another imitated bird sound announced his progress. It was not in his nature to wonder, as he skirted the graveyard, how many more crosses would need to be erected after the inevitable fight between Apaches and whites—or if one would bear his name. He angled away from the rear corner of the building and continued at the same easy pace until he was totally isolated, some hundred yards beyond. He came to a stop at the point where the ground began to rise.

He waited, listening to the trickling spring water and peering up at Chief Ahone and the two braves who flanked him. Then unshod hooves clopped against the rocky ground as the three Apaches heeled their ponies forward. The rope reins were tugged to halt the animals twenty feet away from where the half-breed stood.

With implicit trust in the alertness of their fellow braves ringing the basin, those on either side of the chief ignored the buildings of Santa Luiz to stare challengingly at Edge, their fingers hooked through the trigger guards of the rifles that angled upward from their thighs.

Only the mouth and jaw of Ahone were not shadowed by the broad brim of his Stetson. The mouth was set in a sullen line. "You did well to follow my orders, white eyes. To make my son prisoner was foolish. To allow himself to be captured, he shows himself to be useless hostage. But I would not trade the bravest of my braves for the Apache killer."

Edge nodded. "He said that."

"What else has been said? I allowed you much time with my friends of Santa Luiz. A decision has been made to give me what I ask?"

"The man who killed the Mescalero Apaches with bad whiskey has murdered some whites, too. The stranger who came back here with me is a territorial lawman, Ahone. He plans to see the feller hang."

One of the braves grunted his displeasure.

The chief shook his head slowly from side to side just once, in a manner that suggested sadness as much as a negative response. "How many white eyes he kill?"

"Three."

"His crime against Apaches much bigger. It only right he suffer more than quick death by hanging. You give him to me now." This last was snapped out in the tone of an order.

"No," the half-breed said simply.

148

The brave who had been Ahone's spokesman on the ridge snarled a terse retort in his own tongue.

"Figure you didn't call me anything I ain't been called before, feller."

"We make you our prisoner then," the chief countered, the unshadowed outline of his mouth angry now. But he managed to keep his tone as even as the half-breed's. "Test how long it takes for man who is to die anyway to be handed to us. How many times you have to scream."

Edge curled back his lips to display just the tips of his teeth in a sardonic smile. "The way you feel about Poco Oso, feller? That's about the same as the people in the mission feel about me. I'm all right as shits go, so if I have to go . . ." He shrugged.

"And if we take you, white eyes, the lawman will kill Apache killer? Quick."

"If I die, so do my debts and promises."

"What that means I do not know nor care, white eyes." The angry countenance which was mostly hidden by the shadow of his hat brim, now began to sound in his voice. "But I grow tired of the waiting. And of this talk that leads nowhere."

The flanking braves nodded and grunted their approval.

"It's been a long day and I'm pretty tired myself, Ahone," Edge said, hardening his own tone. He had known there was little chance of the Apaches allowing Larsen to take von Scheel away to be hanged. But because they were

Rancheria Indians, content until now to live by the laws of the whites, it had been worth a try. "So here's the offer. You let the old people go . . ."

The braves snorted their contempt but were forced back into defiant silence by a one-word command from Ahone.

". . . Soon as they're out of this bottom land in the ravine, I'll turn loose Poco Oso. That'll leave just the lawman, me, and the feller you want at the mission. And the way you're so hungry to have him, I figure you'll come try to get him. Just be me and Marshal Larsen in the way."

Now the chief's mouth displayed a sneer. "The Tonto Apaches have not always been at peace with the white eyes land stealers!" he hissed. "In many combats where I have been, our enemies who should become prisoners are just dead. From the single bullet saved for themselves."

Edge nodded. "The old people have no horses. A lot of them are crippled. How far are they going to get if Larsen or me make it a fast end for von Scheel? And you still have it in mind to slaughter your friends because you didn't get what you wanted?"

The two braves did not like the compromise, but they confined the expression of their opinions to sneering looks.

Edge ignored them to peer fixedly at the moon-shadowed face of the chief, who thought deeply about the plan for perhaps ten long seconds.

Finally he nodded curtly. "I agree. Because

of friendship there has been between my people and the white eyes elders of the Mission of Santa Luiz."

Edge thought the clincher had been the promise of the safe return of his son. But Ahone was not about to admit this in the hearing of the grim-looking, angry braves. "I'll start things moving," the half-breed said, and made to turn around.

"I make one condition, white eyes!" the chief said harshly.

Edge remained in a half-turn and cocked his head to one side, quizzically.

"You will place the Apache killer at top of mission tower. So all my braves may see he remains alive." Now the chief's lips parted in an icy smile. "And I think you will agree to this, white eyes. Because you know that after the elders have gone, of the three who remain, the Apache killer will be safest of all. Until you and territorial marshal are dead. Concerned no more."

The half-breed nodded. "It's a deal, feller."

The Apaches wrenched onto their reins to wheel the ponies and then heeled them into a canter up the slope. They were back in their accustomed positions as a link in the encircling chain before Edge reentered the charged atmosphere within the mission church.

"Well?" Larsen asked huskily, the single-word query encapsulating the questions that showed in every pair of the eyes that turned toward the tall, lean man, as he closed the door at his back.

"Some of us have got bright futures," the half-breed answered wryly.

"Damnit, mister!"

"You and me I ain't certain about. But the old-timers are going places. And the drummer, he's going up in the world."

Chapter Twelve

There was a mixed response from the more than fifty people who were crowded into the mission church become hospital–health spa, after Edge was through telling them what he had agreed upon with Chief Ahone. Some of the old-timers started to smile, some to express dismay, and others showed indecision from the moment it was clear they were to be allowed to leave Santa Luiz.

Larsen remained tight-lipped and cold-eyed, alternately closing and opening his fists around the barrel and frame of his Winchester. Fritz von Scheel swayed back and forth, pale and dull-eyed, his Adam's apple rising and falling with the rapid cadence of his breathing. Poco Oso was still unconscious, lying where he had fallen, the blood from an area of broken skin at his temple congealed to an ugly crust.

The German dropped hard to his knees and let his chin fall on his chest in an attitude of total despair, when the half-breed revealed the Apache chief's condition for releasing the old people. And it seemed that every citizen of Santa Luiz began to talk at once after Edge had drawled the words: "There ain't no more to it, so let's get started." He went to where von Scheel was kneeling and hooked a hand under the man's armpit.

"Shut up!" Larsen yelled across the din of voices. And as the noise subsided, he ordered: "Move on out."

Lloyd DeHart and Arnie Prescott were among the group of men and women who needed no more encouragement to shuffle along the aisle toward the doorway. Larsen nodded his satisfaction with this, then glared as muted protests began to be voiced.

"Arnie, you can't!" Amelia Randall called angrily after her husband.

"Easy, Amelia," Phil Frazier urged, his calmly spoken words effectively silencing the new disturbance before Larsen could snarl another order. Then, drawing nods from a few old men and wide-eyed stares of dismay from other of his fellow citizens, he went on: "We can't do it. Not all of us. You're just guessin' about them Thunderhead folks. If they don't show up, there'll just be two of you up against better than thirty Apaches." His good eye constantly looked from Edge, who was heaving the German to his feet, to the unmoving figure of Larsen, and back again.

"You through?" the lawman rasped.

Six men of great age and with a variety of physical disabilities had formed into a close group behind Frazier. Others had fallen back. "We ain't got any weapons, Marshal. But you men got three between you. One of us can use the spare gun. And we can reload. And if anyone gets hit, there'll be another to take his place. For a while."

"You through now?" Larsen said in a harder tone.

Frazier sighed. "Reckon so."

"We're obliged," Edge drawled, as he began to lead von Scheel toward the area at the base of the bell tower. "But you people ain't needed here."

DeHart dragged open the door and called: "Come on. He's said it plain enough, ain't he? Lots of you been prayin' like crazy for him to get back here so as the Injuns'll leave us alone. Iffen we don't do like him and the marshal says, all their trouble's been for nothin'."

He led the way outside, and the group by the door was quick to follow. Then those who had detached themselves from the six who held the same opinion as Frazier, began to drag their feet toward the doorway. Two of them carried the bedridden old woman between them.

Amelia Randall held back to say to the reluctant seven: "That's about the most sense Lloyd DeHart ever did speak, you men. If we stay here to be killed, it'll mean these two young men will be dyin' for nothin'."

Three of the crestfallen old-timers responded immediately to what she said. The others waited for Frazier to nod and turn away.

"We'll be prayin' you're right about help comin' from Thunderhead," he murmured.

Larsen acknowledged this with a nod, then snapped his head around when the unconscious Apache groaned his impending return to awareness. Somebody shouted up to the bell tower that it was time to leave, and the two men who had been on watch came down the adobe steps and hurried out of the building.

Amelia Randall said sadly to the German: "You're a wicked monster, Mr. Von, who maybe don't deserve what these fine men are doin' for you. But I'd be no better than them savages up in the hills if I didn't say God be with you."

"*Danke*," the totally drained and dispirited man murmured.

Frazier shepherded the woman out of the doorway, his good eye threatening to spill the tears that were already coursing down her cheeks. When he closed the door, the sound echoed eerily within the confines of the virtually empty building.

"Don't turn the Apache loose until I get back," Edge instructed, as Poco Oso rolled his head and groaned again.

"I ain't as stupid as you appear to be, mister!" Larsen snarled. He stepped back from the awakening brave and cocked the hammer of the Winchester, angling the barrel down toward him.

"Vhy are you being so stupid, Herr Edge?" von Scheel asked flatly, as he started up the stairway that canted across each tower wall in turn, winding around the well with the bell rope hanging down the center. "A man like you?"

The half-breed did not answer.

"Even if you survive, there vill be no profit for you? And you do not strike me as the kind of man who does things unless there is revard."

"Maybe I'm trying to buy my way into heaven, feller."

"This I do not believe."

"You're right. There ain't enough goodness in the world to buy me that ticket."

The stairway was illuminated by nothing but the moonlight that filtered in through the four arches at the top of the tower, and much of this light did not get past the rim of the big bell that hung from a beam under the tower roof. In the dim light von Scheel stumbled on a broken stair tread and, with his hands tied behind him, would have fallen into the well had not Edge reached forward to steady him.

"You've got the idea, feller," the half-breed said tautly. "But don't get overeager."

"Vhat you mean?" He halted.

"Keep climbing."

They reached the top of the tower, emerging onto a parapet in the west arch, from where they had a bird's-eye view of the straggling line of old-timers moving up the moonlit slope toward the ravine. They could also see three groups of Apaches in menacing attitudes astride their ponies, some aiming rifles at the Mission of Santa Luiz and some covering the exodus, suspicious of a trick. Both Edge and von Scheel did no more than glance at the panorama. Then the prisoner watched as his captor began to haul up the bell rope.

"You tell me now what you mean, *bitte!*"

"Turn around." The half-breed's tone was

even. But his slitted, ice-blue eyes, glinting in the moonlight, made von Scheel do as he was told.

Edge threaded the bell rope between the man's bound wrists and lowered it back down the tower. "You stand right here where you can be seen, feller." Now he gave closer attention to the ridges encircling the basin, ignoring the Apaches below them, as he sought some sign that the men from Thunderhead had taken advantage of the situation. But he saw nothing. "And if things go the way I plan, I'll be back up here to get you sometime. If they don't, you got a choice."

He spat through the archway to the dusty plaza below. "Either way, you're for the high jump." He stepped off the parapet and onto the stairway.

"Herr Edge!" von Scheel sobbed. "The old man spoke of the third gun! Our enemy is mutual! I could be of help if—"

"It wasn't part of the deal, feller. Just keep it in mind that they also serve who only stand and wait."

He continued on down the stairway, aware of the bell rope quivering as the nervous trembling of von Scheel was transmitted to it.

"All set?" Larsen asked from beside the spring, where he continued to keep the Apache covered.

"Just need for the last of the old-timers to make it into the ravine," the half-breed answered as he opened the door and took the makings from his shirt pocket. "Then we turn him loose."

"On your feet and forward, Indian," the lawman ordered. When he had brought the grim Apache to the threshold, he asked: "Light me, too?"

"Figured you'd given them up," Edge said, as he struck a match and ignited the cheroot gripped between Larsen's teeth.

"It's my last one. Been saving it."

"It is traditional among white eyes for condemned man to have final smoke," Poco Oso said flatly, while all three peered across the plaza, past the aspen grove, and up the trail to where the stragglers of the departing old people were still silhouetted darkly against the moon-whitened slope below the flanking walls of the ravine.

"You're beginnin' to irk me, Indian," Larsen growled. "Best you keep in mind that if I kill you here and now, it'll be one less hollerin' savage to aim at when the scrap starts."

"But you will not. You and he, you have too much honor. For this, I respect you. The Apache has greater pride in defeating enemy he respects."

"Be a real pleasure to pay my last ones to you," Larsen muttered.

At last the two men with the bedridden woman moved out of sight into the ravine. An imitated bird call unnecessarily signaled this development to all the Apaches, who were in a position to see it for themselves.

"I go now?" Poco Oso asked, gazing intently but with distrust at the half-breed.

"Make it a rule never to break my word."

The Apache nodded curtly, swung to the

side, and lunged into a run. He crossed the front of the building and then disappeared around the corner to sprint between the side wall and the graveyard.

"He'll tell his pa we're figurin' on help from the Thunderhead men," Larsen asserted.

"If that's going to make any difference, feller, we figured wrong."

"You just gotta be one of the coolest guys I ever did meet, Edge." He did his trick of spitting out of one side of his mouth while the cheroot remained gripped in the other. "Cold as a block of ice, damnit."

The half-breed flicked the part-smoked cigarette out onto the plaza where it landed in a shower of sparks. Then, as Poco Oso began to shriek out a warning in his native tongue, he responded to the marshal: "But by all accounts a hell of a lot harder to see through."

Chapter Thirteen

Edge drew the Colt from his holster and powered himself away from the doorway, angling for the closest house on the south side of the plaza.

The one group of Apaches he could see from his viewpoint slammed their heels into the flanks of their ponies and began a headlong gallop down the slope. Other unshod hooves hit the dusty ground. Other Apache throats gave vent to high pitched war cries.

"I'm stayin' with my prisoner!" Larsen yelled and flung the door into its frame.

The sound of its closing was masked by a fusillade of rifle shots and the barrage of echoes that bounced off the surrounding ridges. Bullets sprayed adobe dust from walls, snagged at the foliage of the aspen grove, and bit into the surface of the plaza.

Edge crashed his shoulder against the door and half staggered into the house, grimacing from the pain of the impact. He paused to get his bearings in the Spartanly furnished household, then veered between the furniture to move less frantically through another doorway to the kitchen, which gave access to the cultivated area at the rear of the house. He crouched at the side of the kitchen window and peered out.

Three groups of Apaches were racing their ponies down the southern slope of the basin, firing only for effect, their piercing war cries counterpointing the cracks of the gunshots.

But there were only seven braves advancing on the cluster of buildings. Two had remained close to the ridge, their eyes watching for the Thunderhead men Poco Oso had warned of, their rifles ready to blast them.

Edge used the Colt to smash a hole in the window, and one of the seven braves threw his arms wide and tipped off the back of his pony, blood spraying from a hole in the side of his head.

Edge's teeth were already displayed in a vicious grin between the drawn-back lips. He snarled through them, "I hope that wasn't just a lucky shot, Larsen," then grunted with satisfaction as another report sounded from the church.

A second Apache was hit, fell from his horse, and lay bleeding from a hole in his back. The attackers had veered away from the line of direct advance and had swung to the side, galloping in a circle around the cluster of buildings well beyond effective revolver range while triggering wild shots from their own rifles.

As he watched, the Frontier Colt silent in his right fist, Edge heard two more shots from within the church. But these were aimed in the opposite direction, and he had a fleeting image of the tall, black-clad lawman whirling away from one window and pumping the action of the Winchester as he raced across the church, then blasting shots from another window.

A dust cloud rose from beneath the pounding hooves of the attackers' mounts, partially veiling the galloping ponies and their whooping, hollering riders. Muzzle flashes streaked the violently shifting cloud, the stench of exploded powder wafting pungently around its vicinity.

The braves who remained as the rear guard up near the ridges moved nothing but their heads, as they searched for the white eyes reinforcements, who Poco Oso had warned were hidden in the rocky hills. Their ponies too were motionless. Their Apache brothers attacking the Mission of Santa Luiz hung low to the sides of their charging mounts and exploded shots from under the necks of the straining animals.

The swirling dust and the speed of the shrieking warriors made it impossible for Edge to estimate the effect Larsen's Winchester was having. He knew only that the lawman was still blasting at the Apaches, could pick out the irregular reports of a rifle fired from nearby from the constant barrage of shooting by the frenzied braves. All Larsen's fire was now directed to the north, while Edge watched the south, having to curb the anger of impatience, as he waited for the circling braves to spiral within effective revolver range.

But this was not to be.

From somewhere up on the high ground, a signal was given. This was seen by a designated brave, and when he sheered away from the circle, the others followed.

Just for a second, Edge was held in the grip of bewilderment that rooted him to the spot, gazing with his narrowed, glittering eyes at the line of Apaches streaming back up the slope. Then he shook himself out of immobility. He swung a leg over the ledge of the smashed window and started into a crouched run the moment he was outside, racing toward the nearest of the two sprawled braves who had been brought down by Larsen's Winchester.

He counted less than twenty braves in the withdrawing line. From above them, he heard the crack of a fusillade of rifle fire, the whine of bullets through the air, and saw spurts of dust close by.

"You're outta your damn mind!" Larsen shrieked.

Edge began to zigzag, cursing when he saw that the rifle of the nearest dead Apache was a single-shot Spencer. It was another ten yards to where the Winchester of the second gunned-down brave lay in the dust. He covered the additional ground, stooped lower while still running, fisted a hand around the rifle, picked it up, and skidded into a turn. He began the same zigzig tactic to get back to cover, ignoring the window to go through the door and crashing his already pained shoulder against it. More Apache bullets pocked the adobe wall of the house, which had already been heavily ravaged during the attack.

He leaned against the inside kitchen wall, breathing deeply, as the rattle of gunfire and thud of impacting bullets diminished and then ceased. Moments later, the sound of hoof beats also ceased.

"Edge?" Larsen called, his tone nervous.

"Quit worrying, feller!"

"Crazy sonofabitch!"

The half-breed pumped the lever action to send an expended shell to the floor and then jacked a fresh round into the breech. "Nothing ventured, nothing gained," he growled softly.

"Oh, sweet Jesus," Larsen said, not much louder than normal conversational level but clearly audible against the trickling of the spring water that was now the only other sound in the stillness of the night. Then he raised his voice to snarl: "Maybe you can go for a couple of Gatling guns next time."

Edge peeled himself away from the wall to peer out through the doorway and leaned around the frame to look toward the ridges to the west. The brutal grin of satisfaction he felt at having claimed the repeater rifle was replaced by a grimace as one of the Apaches up above began to laugh, harshly and scornfully.

"Edge! Larsen! Apache killer!" Poco Oso named each white man in the mission, shouting the words in the tone of obscene curses as he curtailed his laughter. "You are fools to think you can trick the great Chief Ahone! You white eyes are like the smallest of children when you seek to outwit the Apache!"

165

"This is our land, white eyes!" the brave's father yelled, sounding as brutally triumphant as Poco Oso. "Land we know as well as the bodies of our squaws! Fools, as my son called you! Not to know we would guard against such action by men who cannot speak to Apache without lying! Look, white eyes! And prepare to be as our dead brothers are!"

There was the slapping of hands on horse-flesh and the shouting of words to urge the animals into further gallops. Six horses, with shod hooves, were heavily burdened with three riders apiece, unwilling, but unfeeling riders, who were draped over the backs of the animals and lashed in place. They wore no hats, so that as the horses galloped close to the Mission of Santa Luiz, trampled the cultivated plots, and then slowed to pass between the buildings, Edge and Larsen could clearly see that they had been scalped.

"But we didn't hear no shootin'," the lawman said thickly, as if the taste of acid bile were in his throat.

"Knives and lances, I figure," Edge responded, with no need to raise his voice after the horses came to a halt on the plaza, scraping at the ground and snorting their discontent. "Them fellers likely didn't get the chance to draw a pistol or unboot a rifle."

It must have happened in the area of the ravines where he had tried to turn the tables on Poco Oso, he guessed. Maybe just one sentry had been posted there. It would be enough—one pair of eager eyes, watching from a high point for the bunch of unsuspecting whites to ride into the maze of narrow passages. Then a secret signal to bring more braves silently to the expanse of barren, broken land, a brief wait, then a flash of lethal metal weapons. Some screams of fear, some of pain, as honed points and edges bit into flesh. The surprised men from Thunderhead must have been trapped between the rock walls and defenseless against attackers from above. Next came the scalpings and the hauling away of the mutilated dead, to be used by Ahone to whatever advantage presented itself. But not until after his son was either dead or no longer a captive of the white eyes.

"They ain't gonna believe it wasn't our idea," Larsen called bitterly.

"Poco Oso knows it wasn't," Edge replied, "but the way we figured to spring a surprise on them, revenge is going to taste real sweet."

Up under the western ridge, the Indians were forming into a single line of attack. The half-breed counted them and called: "You hit just three to the north, feller."

"Five altogether ain't bad for a guy who ain't a crack shot!" Larsen snarled defensively.

"Not criticizing. Just making sure no Apaches sneaked in close while the rest were giving us the runaround."

"Get some help from you this time, mister? Now you got a rifle?"

"Seems we're all the help we've got, Marshal."

"Set me free and give me a gun!" von Scheel

shrieked, his voice sounding disembodied as it floated down through the moonlit night from the top of the bell tower.

"He could've lent a hand, damnit!" Larsen said bitterly.

"Too late to have second thoughts," the half-breed growled to the lawman at the church window, watching the center of the line of mounted braves to the west, where the city-suited Chief Ahone raised an arm high in the air—then dropped it. "Anyway, you tied his hands."

Only Edge heard his sardonic reply as the thunder of unshod hooves on the slope was almost masked by war whoops that surrounded the Apaches' sense of imminent victory.

"*Bitte, bitte, bitte!*" the helpless and totally exposed German up on the bell tower screamed at the top of his voice.

Edge spat a globule of saliva at the ground as he withdrew into the doorway and muttered, "You and me both, feller."

Chapter Fourteen

This time the Tonto Apaches of the Gallo Rancheria were coming for the kill, galloping flat out in a well-held line until, on a signal from Ahone, they split into two groups, rifles blazing.

Edge neither knew nor cared how Larsen planned to meet the attack and guessed the marshal from Santa Fe had the same attitude toward himself. They were, after all, two against twenty-nine. The odds were hopeless, and in such a situation each was on his own, certain of the fact that he was doomed to die and facing this prospect with the determination to kill as many of the enemy as possible before the weight of numbers won the day. It was better that each white man should fight his private battle, gaining what comfort he could from being aware of the presence of the other but not needing to look out for him.

One half of the attackers angled to the north of the church and the other to the south.

Edge stretched out of the doorway, triggered a shot, and, with the killer's grin parting his lips and narrowing his eyes to slits, saw a brave go off his pony. The Apaches behind him had to veer their mounts around the tumbling body. Then he heard Larsen yell triumphantly, after blasting at the other flank of the attackers. He was not in the church now, but was instead in a house on the side of the plaza opposite to the one which Edge left.

The half-breed waited until the group of Indians swerved their mounts into the gap between the house and the church, slowing them from a gallop and poised to leap off their backs. He came out of the doorway and backed along the rear of the house, his Colt drawn and aimed from the hip. He held the Winchester in the other hand and leveled from the other hip.

Then three braves who had flung themselves to the ground as soon as they rode into cover, came around the corner of the house. They had not expected Edge to be out in the open.

The rifle and the revolver cracked in unison, and two of the Apaches dropped, their faces frozen in death masks expressive of surprise. The third got off a shot with his carbine, but Edge threw himself backward, going under the bullet. He cocked the Colt hammer as he started the fall, squeezed the trigger before his back hit the ground, and the third brave was sent spinning into death with another shot to the heart. All three had a blood-encrusted scalp hanging from his weapons belt.

"One hair-raising moment after another, ain't it?" Edge quipped through his grinning teeth, as he rolled onto his belly, rose to all fours, and scuttled into the gap between the two houses.

Out on the plaza, gunshots exploded in a constant din, the reports echoing off the façades of the buildings and resounding distantly among the encircling ridges. The war cries of the Apaches had the ring of madness to them. Their inbred lust for killing, latent and trapped for the period they had lived on a white eyes controlled Rancheria, now burst to the surface and demanded to be satisfied.

Edge ignored the clamor on the plaza. He had enough experience of Indians in general and the Apaches in particular to be aware of the brand of mass hysteria that had Ahone and his braves in its grip. He had felt something of the same kind himself during the early days of the War Between the States, in battles with the enemy during which the primitive urge to destroy, be it a human being or an inanimate object, had transcended all other considerations—not the least of which was self-preservation.

He used a water butt to get onto the roof of the house that had been his cover. Both guns were cocked and he felt as cool and hard as the metal of the Colt and the Winchester, as he bellied forward over the flat roof, going toward the front of the house.

From here he could see a half-dozen braves, firing and yelling, closing in on the house where Larsen was holed up. It was a sure bet, he thought, that more Apaches were at the rear of the house. From beneath the roof on which he was sprawled, he could hear other highly excited Indians. Still another group, led by Ahone, was running toward the closed door of the church. Up on the parapet of the bell tower, Fritz von Scheel stood like some effigy hewn out of rock.

Edge decided he had no more than a few seconds left to live, and he viewed his impending death with the same icy coldness as he relished the prospect of blasting a bunch of whooping and hollering Apaches into the same eternity whose portals was poised in openness to accept him.

Because what did it matter?

If there was life after death, could its purgatory be worse than so much he had endured in the past? And if the fire and brimstone of the preachers' awesome sermons did not exist? In that case he could use the rest.

He rose to his feet, legs splayed and arms bent at the elbows, resting against each hip. He gripped the Winchester in his left hand and the Colt in his right, angled his rifle toward the Apaches going to get von Scheel, and aimed his pistol at those intent upon killing Marshal Larsen.

He squeezed both triggers simultaneously and thought about his parents. About Jamie. Beth. Would he get to see them again? If he did, Frank Forrest would be around, too. And Billy Seward. Bob Rhett and a thousand other cold-hearted killers, from the war and afterward. For how could a man like Edge get to meet up with his loved ones unless heaven and hell were the same place?

More than two bullets were blasted at the shrieking, milling Apaches on the plaza to send more than half a dozen pitching and rolling to the ground, every agony-inspired movement pulsing a fresh spurt of blood from their wounds.

Those who were not cut down by the fusillade were momentarily stunned, skidded to a halt, and whirled away from their initial objective. Their shock-widened eyes raked from the fallen braves to those others who had survived the vicious hail of bullets. Then they looked frantically at the blank façades of the buildings on three sides of the plaza, and saw the tall, lean, two-gunned Edge on the house roof, grinning as he cocked and fired the Colt again. One-handed, he pumped the action of the Winchester with the stock held tight to his hip by his elbow and triggered a fourth shot. For the better part of a minute, the Apaches were as wildly confused as their ponies, which were rearing and snorting in response to the acrid stink of drifting gun smoke.

Then, as the man on the roof hurled himself down and to the side, moving faster than the two braves who stumbled and fell under the deadly assaults of his bullets, they heard the thud of galloping hooves and the rattle of spinning wheels. For two of them, who snapped their heads around to stare out beyond the aspen grove to the east trail, the sight of von Scheel's wagon speeding toward the Mission of Santa Luiz was the last they ever saw. Another fusillade of rifle shots exploded. Muzzle flashes stabbed through the darkness above the backs of the team, and two of the six bullets that cracked across the plaza blasted into vulnerable flesh.

Edge had decided to abandon his suicidal stand the moment the volley of shots caused him to flick his eyes toward the eastern slope of the basin, where he saw the city-style wagon pitching and rolling down the trail at the head of an elongated cloud of billowing dust. He gave not a thought to the who and the how and the why of the wagon's sudden appearance but simply took advantage of the Apaches' continued confusion to kill two more of them, then dropped flat to the roof. An instant before the no longer triumphant braves wrenched out of their shock and returned fire, some exploding shots toward the racing wagon, others directing a spray of potential death at the roof where Edge had been outlined.

Against the clatter of the now slowing wagon, the crackle of gunfire, the thudding of hooves, the snorting of panicked horses, and the screams of frightened men, the half-breed bellied toward the rear of the roof, thumbing back the hammer of the Colt and working the lever action of the Winchester. He could hear voices in the house beneath him, coming through the smashed window and open doorway of the kitchen. He laid the rifle down beside him, leaned out over the rim of the roof, then folded downward.

Three braves were making to leave the kitchen and go through to the front of the house, fearfully eager to see what was causing the panic on the plaza.

174

Edge had four bullets left in the Colt, and hanging upside down at the top of the doorway, he squeezed the trigger and fanned the hammer, expending the load as fast as the mechanism would allow. He saw two of the braves fall, all three shrieking their terror, then hauled himself out of the doorway, as two bullets cracked through it. With the grin of the pleasure of killing still pasted firmly to his lean, heavily bristled face, he holstered the empty gun, snatched up the rifle, and powered himself into a roll across the roof. He hurriedly checked the area between this house and the next and dropped to the ground.

A gun exploded close by and chips of adobe sprayed into the side of his face. He whirled toward the gap between the rear corners of the houses and saw Poco Oso there. One of the brave's hands was pressed to his belly, blood squeezing out through the cracks between his fingers. In the other was the old Navy Colt.

"Where help come from?" he asked. There was defeat in his face and his voice: the handsome young brave knew he would not have a second chance to kill Edge—that he could not cock and fire his revolver before the aimed Winchester spat death at him.

"Your guess is as good as mine, feller," the half-breed said, as he moved toward the wounded Indian.

The gunfire on the plaza was more sporadic now, and there was less shouting. Poco Oso let his gun hand fall to his side, and he sagged to lean a shoulder against the adobe wall. "You will kill me now?" he asked dully.

"You aimed and missed. I told you about that."

The Apache closed his eyes.

Edge brought the rifle muzzle to within an inch of his chest—left of center—and squeezed the trigger. From such close range, the impact of the bullet sent the corpse backward for at least four feet before it started to fall. The half-breed stepped over it as if it were a heap of trash. He checked the kitchen of the house carefully from the window—to make sure the other two Apaches were dead—before he went inside. There he paused to reload his revolver and listened to the final sounds of battle out on the plaza.

The smile was gone now from his face, which was in the usual impassive set, the urge for killing fully satisfied.

"Mr. Edge? Mr. Larsen? You folks all right?"

The half-breed recognized the voice of the bald-headed Jake Donabie.

"You see any more Apaches that ain't dead?" This was Phil Frazier.

Edge paused again in the parlor of the house to take out the makings and begin to roll a cigarette. Maybe, he thought, the acrid bite of tobacco smoke in his throat would negate the bitter taste on the back of his tongue—a physical sensation born of the emotional turmoil of reflecting upon those moments during which he had been ready to die. *For what?*

"Help me, somebody! Damnit, somebody help me!"

In the stillness between the ringing voices, just the trickling of the spring water marred

176

what would otherwise have been total silence over the Mission of Santa Luiz.

For the opportunity to make others die. That was for what.

Edge spat forcefully, ran his tongue along the gummed strip of paper, completed the cigarette, then stepped into the doorway and struck a match on the frame. As his eyes raked over the scene of the massacre, no sign of emotion showed in a single line of the face that was illuminated in the flare of the match touched to the end of the cigarette.

The wagon had been raced across the width of the plaza and come to rest against the wall of the church at the end of a sliding turn. One of the team horses was dead in the traces, and the other looked exhausted from the struggle to get free. Lloyd DeHart was sprawled across the seat in the total stillness of death. The gaunt John Newman was spread-eagled beside a rear wheel, his goatee stained red by the blood that had gushed from a throat wound. Elmer Randall had not died immediately from the bullet in his chest. There had been time for him to haul himself into a sitting posture against a front wheel of the wagon before his life drained out and left his morose eyes wide open.

Chief Ahone's city suit marked him out clearly among the more than twenty Apaches who were slumped lifelessly on the dusty plaza between the aspen grove and the front of the church. Here and there, a horse carcass lay amid the human corpses. One of them was from Thunderhead and still lashed to its back were the scalped bodies of Jordan and George

Woodin and the massive Ray Hoy—who no longer looked so big. These men, and others from Thunderhead who, like them, were rigid and long dead, had great patches of congealed blood surrounding the deep wounds in their backs.

All the horses were motionless, heads hung low in the aftermath of panic. The only movement Edge noticed on the moonlit plaza, as his glinting eyes surveyed through the curling smoke of his cigarette, was in front of the house immediately opposite. There the black-clad marshal sagged drunkenly in the doorway, sideways-on to Edge, in such a way that the half-breed was able to see the knife that was sunk to the hilt in the center of the lawman's back.

Then the one-eyed Phil Frazier showed himself in the doorway of the church, Jake Donabie beside him. Both of them held Winchester rifles as they, like Edge, surveyed the moon-shadowed buildings for Apaches who had survived. Two other old-timers, whom Edge recognized without knowing their names, stepped out from between houses. They also had rifles.

"We done for them all, Phil," one of these men called.

Larsen groaned, slid down the door frame, and came to rest as a still and silent heap on the threshold of the house. Edge started toward him, then turned away, to head for the aspen grove. The rifle was canted to his shoulder, and he drew the razor from his neck pouch. A glance up at the bell tower showed that von Scheel was still standing on the parapet, seemingly petrified by the fear he had experienced while looking down upon the slaughter.

"We felt so helpless, Mr. Edge," Frazier said in a melancholy tone, as Donabie moved out of the church doorway to check that the men sprawled on and near the wagon were as dead as they looked. "It was Lloyd DeHart reckoned we oughta see if maybe the drummer had a rifle aboard his wagon. Turned out that female stuff was just one line he carried. Two cases of brand new Winchesters and three crates of shells hid under all that fancy stuff."

Edge used the razor to cut through the ropes that lashed three corpses to the back of a strong-looking black gelding. The rigid bodies fell heavily to the ground, not shifting at all from their folded-over positions. There was blood crusted and blackened on the saddle, but the half-breed ignored it as he swung astride the horse and slid the Winchester into the empty boot.

"Had a lot of volunteers to come give you and the marshal a hand," Frazier went on. "Folks appreciated what you done for them. But couldn't properly fit any more on the wagon."

Edge nodded and looked up at the German drummer: "Seems you're a man of many parts, feller!" he called.

"A lot of them private!" Frazier growled. "Bet he figured to sell these rifles to the Apaches." He tossed the Winchester away.

179

"You leavin' already?" Donabie asked miserably, after discovering the Santa Luiz old-timers were as dead as they looked.

"Got some money waiting for me in Tucson."

The gelding beneath him was eager to leave the plaza and the stink of stale gun smoke and spilled blood.

"I'll let the others know it's okay to come back," Frazier growled, as he swung into the church.

Larsen gave a low groan and raised his chin off his chest. The mark of death was written into every line of his darkly bristled face. "Edge," he croaked. "I ain't gonna be able to take him back to Los Alamos." There was a plea in every word that struggled out of his slack mouth.

Then Frazier jerked on the bell rope. The German was hit in the back by the rim of the bell and plunged off the parapet. He did not scream as he tumbled into mid-air. But Frazier uttered a cry of alarm as the rope was wrenched from his hands by the plummeting weight of von Scheel. Then the end of the rope around the man's bound wrists snapped a moment before he crashed into the top of his wagon and smashed through it. Cartons were crushed and bottles were shattered under the impact that killed the man.

"What was that?" Larsen gasped, trying in vain to turn his head.

Edge twisted in the saddle to look up the east trail toward the ravine. Amelia Randall was at the head of a group of old-timers, trying to hurry on aged legs, desperately anxious to find

180

out how many loved ones and friends had died in the battle of Santa Luiz. All the while the encircling ridges continued to echo distantly with the two-note call of the bell.

Ding . . . dong.

"Like the lady might say it, feller," the half-breed answered Larsen as the sweet smells from the smashed perfume containers in the wagon filled the plaza. "That was a Von falling."

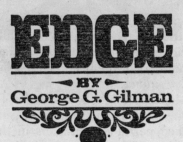